THE ART of OUR MELODY

"The True Love of Withered Flowers"

RAJESH RAJAVELU

ISBN
Paperback 978-9-33415-289-0
Hardcase 979-8-89906-931-4

Cover Page Design by Akhilesh HP & Rajesh

Praises for the Novel

"A shy boy meets a lively girl. Sparks fly instantly. What happens next? A cute love story pans out well between the pages of this book. An enjoyable read" - Megha S, author of **"By Two Coffee"**

"A book that can make you forget and put you amidst the characters. A book of details and art." - Rudresh Jayaram, author of **"Blooming Chaotically"**

"The strings of melody can be heard while reading the book, the book is apt for people who like to weave moments of passion and vulnerability. Each page encapsulates the raw emotions of love, innocence, and vulnerability and the readers are in for a whirlwind." - Maha Fatima, author of **"21 Emotions"**

"I'm tempted to buy a new violin which will eventually become melody of my life. That's the impact of Rajesh's Work" - Nagarjun, Art Enthusiast.

Acknowledgement

As a debut author, I especially want to thank my parents for encouraging me to pursue my passion from a young age. Still, I recall that the first poem I wrote was posted on my school's notice board in fifth grade. The adventure began there, and I would like to thank my school for guiding me in the right direction. And my sincere gratitude to my dad, mom, sister and cousins who strive me to grow and help me in every possible moment, a blessing in my life.

Without my friends, this book would not be possible. I am grateful for their companionship and inspiration who have stood by me through thick and thin. I struggled financially while writing this novel, but they eventually offered their shoulders. Every second, I owe their affection.

And I'm thankful to my school bench pals, who asked me to make up an amusing story with them to pass the last 10 minutes before departing for the day.

In particular I want to acknowledge Rudresh Jayaram, an author and poet who guided me and has been my instructor and motivator. I couldn't have written this book without him. I'd like to wish him the best of luck in whatever future awaits.

I'm deeply grateful to my editor Megha who supported me by editing this book with her enormous skill, precision and with commitment. I'm fortunate to work with her.

Akhilesh, my cover designer and my proof readers deserve my thanks who helped me timely to complete this project. Many thanks for supporting me.

And my sincere thanks to my colleagues who always encouraged during this journey and most of all I want to thank my great supporters who motivated me with their kind hearted words.

Do you know what love is?
I asked plenty of fish in the sea. Still, I couldn't find a
dictionary that describes the real meaning of love. Often,
I used to search in nature, as it tells our story, reminds us
of our bond and connects our emotions.
Moreover, ***what is love?***

Before:

Love is the fundamental imperative to lead a happy life. It serves an intent for the society, family and for self-being. Spreading love and happiness is not a gift from our birth, it's difficult to edify among everyone, as it will be led by a person's interactions, understanding and the set of values defined in their surroundings. Imagine-
The earth without gravity,
The sea without water,
And the sun without its shine.
No creature in this ecosystem will survive. Of course, every fauna without love is incogitable.

The authentic love of gravity will never reduce on the earth. If yes, it will be the last day to attract its bond, it may fail in its own cluster. Yet, it will exist as a different form in other galaxies. Love is immortal and invisible.

"Learn"

"Learn to gratify"
"Learn to spread the serenity"

Chapter-1

First Love

My first love, Padma. The lady with charming, long thin straight hair, hazel brown eyes in a rounded face. She is a good hearted one in a world of uncountable stars. Courage is a part of her personality. And the love she has towards her child is endless and unconditional. Her lap is the safest place to sleep and to unwind my heart.

For me, she shines like the stars even in the day. She is my world and my happiness.

In my universe, she is...
The pure pearl,
With the fullest heart.
The pure soul,
With the fullest generosity.
She shines all over, by
Adding pebbles to my pot,
And water to my root.

She raised me with her courage, kindness and her finest love. As her admirer, I always try to walk and follow her path.

I still remember the occasion of my 12th birthday (August 20), my mom in an elegant white saree with golden lines, gleamed like an angel without feathery wings and was inviting everyone with her warmth and bright smile. The place was cheerful with beautiful people and their silent anticipation. I wore new blue trousers, a round necked white T-shirt and a short sleeve with a furious Spider-man's picture. The balloons were decked in vibrant colors. All my elders were engaged in serving snacks and juices to the guests.

My eyes were on the ball of vivid red cherries, half hidden in the cake and half sticking its head out. After seeing the gallery of spectators, I was doubting myself whether I would get those cherries or not, but I had a bait in my eyes to catch them fiercely. In time, my mom came near me to start the bash. Cheers of love started,

"Happy Birthday to Mathav."

"Happy Birthday to Mathav."

The blessings elated my heart. Being a recipient of everyone's love is bliss. I was delighted and started to show all my 28 teeth vibrantly forgetting that I hadn't brushed properly that morning.

After cutting the cake, my mom fed me a small piece with one cherry on the top. Finally, I could get the lovable cherries. It was a long wait for the kiddish satisfaction. Following that, everyone was busy stealing a slice of cake and hunting cherries. It was the chaotic part of my birthday celebration.

Thereafter, I started to run in and out of my home without any reasons. Shortly, my mom called me with her pleasing tone. "Mathav,"

"Yes Mom" I shouted.

"I got you a big gift Mathav, come fast!" she smirked. I ran like a small bolt of thunder towards my mom.

She held a big rectangular cardboard box in her pretty hands. I had no idea what it was as it was wrapped. She handed it to me and asked me to unbox it. My excitement was over the moon, my face was like Motu for his samosa, thinking that the box would be full of chocolates and cookies. What was it? What was it? The anticipation was getting to me. Soon after, unwrapping the box from covered bubble sheets, I squealed "Mom, Violin?"

"Violin" the rosewood tail heads, glossy finish shone like lights in my eyes. In the heat of excitement, my heart leapt over the tempo and a rhythm sprung in my joy. The dynamics of my body were out of control. Mom asked, "Do you like it?"

With a big smile on my face, I nodded ardently.

It was the first surprise gift in my life. It's been in my heart till date and has touched me deeply. After unboxing, I handed it to my mom and asked her to play some music.

She is a violin virtuoso. On every occasion, all my family members eagerly waited for her performance so that she would own the stage like always. To an applause and a quest of evoking everyone's emotions, she started to play "My Heart Will Go On" composed by James Horner. Promptly, thousands of butterflies started to fly in my stomach. I was unclear, clueless and had no inkling about the blissful notes and the melody. I used my proprioception (7th Sense) to track the magic of my mom.

My eyes were fully focused on the bow and the bridge, thinking of the miracles.

It was the first time I heard that tune play. As it started, my heart was touched and I ended up with tears. Yes, music has a bond of attraction and evokes happiness beyond boundaries. I waited eagerly for the end, to cuddle my mom. After three minutes of her soulful magic, I ran fast with my happy tears. I hugged her blindly and expressed my kiddish love. The art of her music filled everyone's heart.

In a stammering voice, I said, "Mom, Love You!" "Thank you for this amazing gift."

She replied with an adorable kiss on my forehead, wiped my tears and asked,

"Mathav, why are you crying? I'm here!"

I gazed for a few seconds at her loving eyes. I was comfortable in my silence and could not verbalize my emotions.

"Mathav, okay, here is your new friend,

Learn….

Learn to gratify and

Learn to spread the serenity"

"In the later stages of my life, I understood that whenever I'm lending my ears to beautiful music, my heart beats with the melody and my eyes precipitate the rain in the form of love, unknowingly and apparently. The reason is intangible, as it's connected to my inner serenity."

She knew that I would stand out in the crowd and I won't blend in with anyone. I love the way she made me complete with my new friend and to transpire from my solitary world. Desperately her therapy worked in my later life.

On the same day, around 5 p.m. I sat on the window pane, rested my head against it and dreamt of a situation of me playing the violin. Her musical magic was such that it was quite difficult to get out of the moment. My mind persisted to learn fast. By staring at the pages of the clouds, I was completely oblivious to everything. Curiosity was just building up in my head.

Where are these clouds roving?

Was there any end?

Suddenly, my friends shouted in an energetic voice. "Hey! Mathav, come let's play; Hide and Seek." I grinned and jumped down, without reading the last page of the clouds.

In the airy evening, we gathered with excitement in our little garden, and were ready with our pledging hands. But it was for "Odd man out." The sequel started with the five of us, then four, then three of us, and ended with me.

Aarav with his giggles said,

"Mathav, you're out, you should find us." With my pleading smile, I insisted, "Aarav, you will be the first!"

He was embarrassed for a moment and smiled widely, "Let's see, Mathav."

I closed my eyes so tight against the darkness of the gate at the wall. After counting backwards from twenty to one, I shouted, "Boys, I am coming down!" and I opened my eyes, scanned the yard, looked for sounds and movements. There was a silence around, I lifted my head and checked all the tree branches, no one was around. In my deep search with eyes like binoculars, I found a foot peeping from behind the big pots of plants. Walking with gumboots on the grass, I reached near the pot from the other end.

I found Arun sprawled on the ground, his heart pounding in anticipation. I stifled my laughter and with a loud voice, I shouted, "Arun! I found you!"

Then, everyone jumped to the centre with big relief. We enjoyed tagging each other, hiding near the house gate and the big trees of our garden. The moments of childhood were always memorable. The laughter, the friendship and the joy of games. Suddenly, the clouds formed against us, thundered, and stopped us by pouring its showers. We ran fast back home, shouting "Come fast! Run! Run!"

I scrambled to my shelter, to my window. I started to watch the play of rain. The birds were chirping and the melody of love was on the trees. Quickly, my heart was thrilled by the excitement and I was reminded of my new friend. I sprinted inside my room, took my violin and started to play with the bow. I couldn't bear those unpleasant sounds that were created, hanging without the rhythm which cracked my eardrum for a minute.

I decided to learn the medium of evoking joy and emotions through music. After my dinner, seeing the violin on the right side of my bed, I slept peacefully.

The day went well with happy moments, filled by the evening rains and throughout the day I was excited with the joy, blessings and my mom's gift.

The next day, after school, I ran to my mom with my new friend to kick start the friendship. She took me to the outdoor garden where I could enjoy learning with the melodies of nature. Under the thousands of adorable clouds, perennially blooming tree, crowded by the green enchanting leaves. She started to teach me from the basics, how to hold the bow, posture techniques, how to set left-hand fingers and so on.

Time passed, I'd say frankly, there was no sturdy efforts from my end in the initial days. I would listen very less but think and dream about the result rather than learning and enjoying the process. I certainly thought not to quit, owing to the fact that it is my best friend and I wanted to make it foremost in my life. A week later, while she was teaching, in a bit of chariness, I spoke out, "Mom! I'm finding it too difficult to play good music, but I never want to give-up. The sense of fear is building up whether I can make it? Whether people will listen to my music or not?"

She understood that I was struggling to learn. She replied, "Mathav, learning music is the most beautiful experience, initially it might be challenging. But if you stay calm and with the proper practice, you'll get better soon. You need to dedicate yourself to the process of learning to stand out from all. Foremost enjoy and love the process, remember that every good musician started from the stage where you're now! Moreover, I'm here, Mathav."

After that, she designed the method meticulously, where I could capture the techniques comfortably. Day by day, week by week, I felt the stages of improvement and growth in my journey. She never hesitated even after thousands of mistakes. I never hesitated in correcting them too, because she used to tell me to learn from the mistakes.

After 8 months of regular practice, I learned the level of confidence to rule my kingdom. I got a chance to light up my place on the occasion of my mom's 35th birthday (April 2nd). In the late evening, the occasion was arranged. Under the dark sky, yellow lights glowing. Elegant pink balloons and streamers dancing on the walls, blue fairy lights showered around the windows. In spite of it all, my mom's face was glowing and shining with her refined gratitude. Among many angels, she looked most resplendent in spreading smiles. As an auspicious sign signifying everyone's good health, she wore a pink saree, adorned with the simple silver and gold zari, matching the graceful space.

Since morning, I waited avidly for the cake cutting, so I could get some of my favorite cherries. This time, it was so bitter and there were no cherries in the cake. Apart from that, I was so keen to showcase my past 8 months of friendship in the gathering, because everyone would hear my heart beat without any stethoscope or the image of a cardiograph. Music, the medium of gratifying love and emotions.

After the cake cutting and the mandatory scoop on the plate, the time for my music arrived. I was quite nervous to play in front of everyone. The presence of my mom beside me amplified my confidence and comforted my strings. Surrounded by silence and with a deep breath, I reminded myself of my love for music, and I raised my friend to my chin. I drew my bow across the strings. I held my breath and started his soulful gushes. For a minute, I played the small note by his strongest bond and ended with some fiddling.

-About Fiddling, she is good at fiddling. Whenever she plays, my heart flies like it has wings. She creates an energetic space which will reverberate with everybody. Ofcourse, there is plenty of joy in her faster pieces.

After my play, the place was lightened more and more by the glow on everyone's face. The claps felt like I was dancing on the moon. The dark part of the iris in everyone's eyes was sparkling and the radiance had spread among hearts. I felt it was extremely complicated to measure in terms of the lux. I could see the eyes of my mom swelled by love. My perfect gift for the evening. She hugged and held my tiny face in her warm hands. In the silence of the moment, When I was looking into her strong eyes, she kissed my bubbly cheek. And finally, my heart let out a breath of relaxation.

She expressed her love by, "Mathav! You enchanted us, it was too beautiful to hear! Your melody mesmerized us!"

In coyness, I nodded, "Thank you, Mom."

Still, I'm thinking of myself as an introvert guy. How did I come in front of so many people and play music? To perform in front of an audience, the artist needs a good amount of firmness to transpire, either to hold the mic or to deliver their art. But there is no question when it comes to gratifying others. That's what I learned from my mom. My heart goes impulsively by taking all her courage and the closest arms of my friend to face any adventurous stage. Then frequently, I started to play in order to energize everyone in my home on every occasion.

Day by day, Year by year, the bond of our friendship had been growing like the salt and the sea.

We will bring tides to shower happiness,
And happiness to reduce the stress of the body.

We are the home for millions of species,
Dive deep for the soul's serenity,
Breathe slowly for exhaling the grace.
Walk widely for the new horizon.

For almost years, I've been using the same 3/4 violin, gifted by my first love. Do you want to know more about our friendship? Ask the dust, it weeps daily that it was failing to rust my heart. Even Dust questioned me?

All I could say was, "My friendship is the medium of gratifying everyone's emotions, to heal their tears in the form of music and to spread peace and kindness among everyone's heart."

Yes! Now, ***I'm a violinist too***.

I failed to reach esteem,
In lack of belongings and love,
I failed,
I failed,
And I failed.

Chapter-2

24ᵗʰ Birthday

Just pause the running life.
If you're growing in life, turn a mirror and observe, it is blinded by an unseen coat and you are going to lose something behind one side of the wall, to look graceful and to glow on the other side, that is life. This phase of life is uncertain and unpredictable.

While flying beneath the sky, there was less density. When I grew up, the density became heavier and heavier to sustain. My school and college life were withdrawn from the social world and that of friends, I craved the life that basic people have, but the reality hit me differently in my early stage. My purpose in life was to serve gratitude and love. That's how I had grown up and my mother taught me. But everyone else was pretentious and it didn't help the cause.

I didn't find the truth and love. It ended with being bullied by peers and I struggled to energize my mind and my health. Then of course, I was lost in the space of solitude. But, the words of my mother were my sole motivation, I was driven and they were still driving me! The words from her book are so precious, I never let them fade or smudge with time. As a constant, it is the beautiful frame in the wall of my heart and I am hooked by the golden wired nails.

I'm Mathav. A software Engineer, studied as an average student, worried a lot about the future and possessed the typical teenager anxiety. The clouds were passing but I couldn't find the last page of it. The stories of my life were incomplete.

During my college days, I desired that my job should be in the Southern part of India. I don't know why. I felt cozy and comfortable. As per my desire, from the college placement, I got a job in one of the big MNC's as a Junior Analyst. With a mix of nervousness and excitement and a small backpack on my shoulder full of dreams, I stepped into the big city of (Bangalore) from a lane by holding hope in my hands.

Bangalore, the beauty. Vibrant with a heart of greenery around the seamless landscapes, the peerless weather, bustling streets and the shining skies spread all over the day. The sun rises and sets around the big towered buildings to remind us, Bangalore is here! Indeed, there is a lot we can achieve in this city. The narrow roads for wide opportunities and every corner is seized with new possibilities and adventure.

With the encouragement of a welcoming city, I uplifted my vision and believed that I'm on the right path of my journey. Unexpectedly, I found a paying guest accommodation for an affordable rent in Indiranagar. It is quite difficult to find an accommodation where both the food and stay go hand in hand in a well-organized manner. Sometimes, any one of those had to be compromised. My colleagues would mention that their stay was regrettable and often lacked all the basic needs. I was lucky by the way.

The days were passing like evening clouds. Going to the office with complete excitement about achieving something big and returning with a loss of energy. Initially everything was challenging. Later on, it all turned obvious. My colleagues were really kind hearted with a healthy state of mind, energetic and lovable too. Never showed their frustration and they thought of me as a well-suited man for the corporate world…

In The brightness of wider skies,
The chirpy sounds, made me feel over the moon,
Bonds trapped in the full joy of springs,
Aerial roots are up reared my Life,
And Seasons never lasted…

But still, I couldn't find any open place to gear my heart. I often stayed quiet and just replied to their talk. "Me time" is always resilience from loneliness and to unwind my mind. Nevertheless, I had my close friend who was immortal in his own way-*Violin*. Sometimes, I thought,
Whether the creation of my soul was meaningless?
You can ask me, why?
And my only answer is "Yes"

Because, neither my question nor my stories were answered and probably it would never be from this universe. As a result, the state of being alone was my only retort.

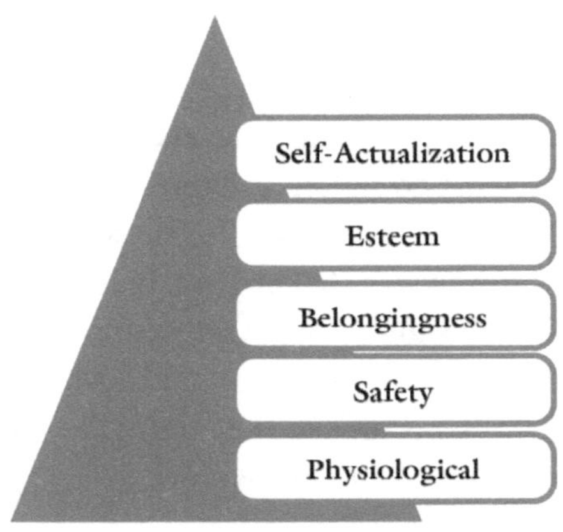

Maslow's Hierarchy of Needs

According to Maslow's Hierarchy of needs, my life was hanging in the bottom with only basic needs. Every human being in this universe has a goal to reach the highest level of hierarchy, but

I failed to reach esteem,
In Lack of belongings and love,
I failed,
I failed,
And I failed.

For more, I'm reserved and have absolutely very few acquaintances. My close circle was my friend (Violin) and my mom. I lost my 23 years in a state of solitude.

Then imagine how my heart pounded on seeing the innumerable friends on the roads, parents showering love on their kids in the parks, warm hugs of elders and sharing shoulders of couples.

I jumped completely into the new universe,
Out from all, dived into the wide space,
My heart is yearning for an intimacy,
Craving for love,
Longing for care……

Sorry! Sorry!
(Just give me a minute, let me wipe my tears).

I almost cried every night with my friend by supporting my head on his strings. He healed all my emotions and hugged me with the peace of his melody. I always thanked my pillow for soaking up all my tears and covering my eyes till they ceased.

"Just stop crying Mathav! Nothing will change, until you change your perspective." This constantly served as a mental reminder to begin each day.

Today, my 24th birthday. Because of the few acquaintances I had, there were no wishes, no greetings and no celebrations. I never craved love in the past 23 years, I was in the world, completely isolated from unknown human faces, cultures and habits. After moving to this new world, things were totally different and every

corner influenced me to crave for it. It feels too difficult to spend each minute of the day in my office. No smile on my face, no strength in my walk. The reality of my life hit hard that there is no soul in this world to pamper me, wish me, bless me and hug me. The day without these feelings seems like it is throwing questions.
Why am I born in this world?
What is the reason behind it?
Am I expecting something big in this world?

Anyone! Please slap my face and wake me up from the expectations. Teach me the reality. I cry alone. I don't know why I'm like this. Is my birth cursed? I feel mentally ill. But a part of my heart says,

The sweet is too salty,
Nurture yourself,
To Accept,
The Sweet is just salty…….!!

As evening progresses, to unwind my mind I walk to my second home (the Temple). I believe in God, who listens to my voice apparently, without any expectations underneath this paradise. In 700m from my home, there is a sacred place - a Shiva temple. Hundreds of worshippers and theists were streaming out daily with different hopes and reasons. I was definitely one among them, but I was not a daily visitor. In the softening evening, streets are dimming even with the lights, people take restless walks on the roads at the end of a tiring day to rest.

While heading towards the temple, again my heart pounds with a question, why am I born? It stresses my mind and seeks an answer.

As I reach, I sit near the pillar where I can see the sanctum (Garbhagriha) and the rhythm of everyone's life getting slow inside the holy place. The temperature of every cell drops apparently under his shadow. The silence is healing. It is like medicine to witness the almighty even without his appearance. There are thousands of thoughts crossing from my left brain to right and again right brain to left, that leave me puzzled. Thousands of thoughts!! Which are untold and hidden.

In the trapped thoughts,
I'm falling towards the trash,
Am I lost in my vision?
In my gloomy sky,
I'm huddling under my shadows,
Are my days being worse?

My eyes are covered with the smog of tears with the drifting hopes and lack of belongings. It is too difficult to console me. Unable to put up a happy face. I cry inside, looking at my god, hoping that he will pamper me and wish me for my birthday. Silence is the only reaction from him. But I trust in him, that he will never create an environment where I will fall. Indeed, he will help me to hold on to the big hopes and make me trust in life.

All of sudden, a small hand of God rises and calls behind my shoulder. Quickly, my heart pounds back and forth, the soft skin touches my heart. I hold my breath for a second. In the moment of excitement and in the inflated anticipation. I turn my head. I am stunned, "Oh My Goodness." I have never seen the face of God. Yes! two beautiful eyes, chubbiness on the cheeks and an alluring smile. Here! The cute baby in the red skirt, with an immense prettiness in her presence.

She hands me the two coins which fell from my pocket while sitting. I grab those slowly in her beautiful gaze. With a grin, I smirk "Thank you, pretty!" She nods with a graceful smile.

Without any words, the love of that cute girl enamors me in a fraction of a second. I felt so blessed to receive from her, like it's God's beautiful gift for my birthday. With her smile and presence, she stole my little heart and healing my untold pain. I ask God, "please don't go! stay with me." But she walks away from the temple by holding the hands of her grandma.

The peace of a smile on her face,
Brought my inner serenity.

Her power in the eyes
Convincing me,
That the world exists!
Nothing is permanent in this world,
And nothing is to lose.

She reminds me of hope,
And self-love for my life.
Yes, God Exists!!

With a newfound hope and the beautiful gift, I happily step out from the temple by controlling my legs, which are doing the happy dance on the road. Now, in my eyes the streets are shining by the yellowish lights, soothing in the sounds of air and trees are heavenly, flowering the bliss, The newly altered eternal bliss.

After my dinner, I usually take a walk for tea around 10.30 p.m. A perfect tea lover. My love of tea never ends. If you ask me, whether I have it 5 times per day? I can say, "No, 5000 times per day." Ya, It's too much, But sorry…... There is a small tea shop near my home on 100 ft road. It's the most happening place for chai, where we can see a lot of adolescents with a cup of tea in one hand and a lot of dreams to share on the other hand. They share sleepless nights to enhance the glow of Chai Days. The quote for Chai on the wall, hails me regularly,

"YOUR CHAI
And Chai Keeps a Check
on Your Immunity, Energy,
and All Things That
Keep You Moving.

After buying my favorite "Regular Elaichi chai." I sat in a corner near the stamped green grass wall to enjoy the vibe of night city when it was drizzling. Every sip of my love, energizing with its aromatic pleasure, is warming my taste buds. It is the perfect digestive aid for my happy life.

Soon after, a sleek green Lamborghini, roars with its engine power; the stylish color drew my eyes towards left, the echo of power abiding the space, reverberating everyone's heart and flew with the speed of air. The engineering miracle caught everyone's attention for a minute. With a feeling of curiosity, I turn my head towards the right. The yellow lights flashed in my eyes like thunder, flicking for a second to welcome the most admiring and enchanting woman of this world with an umbrella in her hand. The wind transits away for her in every gait. The time of 10.48 p.m. freezes for a minute. The complete universe is against us, as everyone loses a minute of life. *The minute of my life.*

Every step of her walk, graces my heart and lets my inner child out to peek at her without taking my eyes off. My heart smiles at the magic of her ecstasy. Holding a book in her hand, she walks slowly to the counter and with a cup of tea, she takes a seat opposite to mine. Her black kurta and the white pants had the magic of a classy look. Her pose embodied the courage of Indian women. I love the way she is. My eyes lost control and peeked at the first sight.

My soft breath carried the melody of love and the harmonic rhythm of waves moves across her neck and shoulder. The soft stone of her earrings starts to jiggle to my heartbeat. Her curled hair leaps at every scale. With this image, she looks completely the prettiest woman in the world. With every sip of tea, she pulls all my breath and unwinds my emotions. Reflecting deeply on that, I feel she is my girl, my love. *The love of my life.*

She lifts up her cute gaze at me. There are no words in the world to express my happiness. My inner child yearns for me to go and have a conversation with her, but the maturity of my mind is stopping me and reminding me of the fear of vulnerability and turbulence.

I feel happy with the mix of hope by seeing her, Ya! Just by seeing her. She left soon after the beat of my melody ended. I never felt those butterfly movements in my life. I question the light, which has shown me the attraction of her fetching rays,
Is it love? Or just infatuation?

Again, the lights flick by saying that, "It's a profound impact of the emotions." I had no comeback to that. I felt, she is my "Ammu."
The name which I desired to call my love, the expression of my affection and the trust.

I left the shop with the memories of her elegance and with those fleeting moments. The day was entirely surprising, I felt blessed by the pretty girl and happy with the smiles of my cute "Ammu." My little hope says that I will definitely meet her soon.

Next day at the same time, I walked with hope to see her and I waited for some time. I failed to notice her presence. Then, I ask the street lights to spark the gleam on her fairy earrings. He fails to make me grin, as she did not show up. While returning, my search for her continued under all the street lights of Bangalore.
"Where is my Ammu?" The love of my life.

My search for her,
Morning in my bed,
Hand with a towel,
Wiping and drying my head.

My search for her,
As a feather on my breakfast table,
Nourishing with love,
And in the cute hugs to start my day.

My search for her,
Under the thousands of skies,
Sitting on my bike,
And guiding me to cross all the pits of my life.

My search for her,
On my office floor,
In the essence of my tea,
And while returning from work.

My search for her,
Again, in my fairy dreams,
And in the peace of my sleep.

In search for her,
My next morning……

My search for her even in my dreams! It's been 5 months since the day I saw her first, but still my search for her is a never-ending story.

One fine day, during the office break, the discussion was about everyone's hobbies. I had a silent presence at the corner of the table. Rahul, my teammate, the energetic boy, who mingles with everyone in my office was also seated. The talkative idiot of my team. Yes, everyone makes fun of him and moreover, he makes fun of everyone. But no one hurt others in any way. It showed the healthy state of my colleague's mind.

He starts the conversation with his hobbies, exploring new places and talking with them about culture, food, art and their beliefs. It seems new to me but I liked it. By following him, all my teammates started to share their hobbies like watching movies, playing cricket and reading books and so on.

Finally, the arrow pointed at me, the focusing eyes of everyone, expecting something different and creative. I just twirled my head among everyone and stayed quiet for a second. Rahul, with his energetic voice egged me on,

"Hey Mathav, what you are thinking?"

I whisper slowly that, "Nothing much guys, I love music and playing Violin."

Janu, the cute chirpy girl of my team excitedly asks, "Do you play Violin?"

In my slow monotone, "I do," I smirk.

Then Janu adjures, "Huh! Then definitely you should play for us!"

"Ya! But you should sing." I tug her.

Suddenly, Rahul with a grin on his face said, "I can't bear her normal voice, if she sings, that's going to be our last day." Giggles followed for a moment.

Janu stiffens and screams with her chirpy voice, "You Idiot, Insane." chuckles continued.

"Mathav, I know a place for jamming session. There will be a big gathering of artists and music lovers with complete positive energy. You should definitely go there, Mathav. I'm sure you'll be excited."

"Ya, it feels something interesting."

"Mathav, you know! The session is every Wednesday night. Let's go next week and you should bring your violin, what do you say?" he pulls my leg.

"Rahul, I'm not interested in playing among the big group, maybe in our next team outings, I will play for you guys!"

"Mathav, it's a great platform to share your experiences. Definitely, you will enjoy it. Come, don't think too much, Let's have fun!!" He tries to convinces me.

"Okay," I nodded.

Then, Rahul quips, "And Janu, you are welcome, but please don't try to sing."

"Get lost, Idiot."

Our group pushes us.

Then, I asked Rahul, "Where is it?"

He said, "Lahe-Lahe" (*The home for every artist*).

The moment of excitement starts in the corner of my heart, imagining myself in the group playing violin.

Soon, we leave with a hilarious talk among ourselves. But my search for her continued, from every morning to night and again,

In search for her,
My next morning!

Don't fall on the roads,
Take my infinite heart,
And fill your love.

Chapter-3

The Music Night

The shades of colorful Bangalore changing from dark night to dawn. The lights of hope glitching my eyes. My friend is at the corner of my table reminding me about evening jamming sessions. The essence of early morning rejuvenates my longing. And today, Wednesday. The day to cherish the melody. Quite excited about the evening, I made the plan to be at my office early, so I could head out soon for the evening melodies. The day as usual goes in search for her under all the clouds.

In the office, during morning break, the excitement in Janu's eyes jumps from her upper eyelids and lands on her lips to ask, "Mathav, Are you ready for today's session?"

I nod, "ofcourse"

"Janu, who is your favorite musician?" I lift my question to understand her choice of music.

After deep thinking, "she replies, ARR."

"Nice" I smirk.

Her excitement again jumped from her lower eyelids and she questioned, "What about you?"

"Janu, my love for music is different from others. To answer you exactly, you can be my favorite musician.

Perhaps, if you play the rhythm of your breath. I love music, just the music." I filled the gap.

Rahul raises his chin, "Mathav, you sound totally different, I have never listened to this kind of a statement even from big rockstars."

"My pleasure, Rahul." I smiled.

Janu with her chirpy melody, "Mathav, I think with this statement, even before listening to your melodies, you made me your fangirl. None of the artists does this, you are totally different Mathav, we're blessed to have you."

"Thank you, Janu. I hope we will have a good time today." I replied and saw the glee in Janu's eyes.

Rahul reminds us, "Guys, be on time. Janu, especially you, don't try to bring last-minute excuses. Instead of those, bring your makeup kit, you can save enough time." Everyone chuckles,

"Rahul. First, you be on time." she screams. He squabbles, "Let's see who is gonna be late."

Alex adjures, "Rahul and Janu, stop your childish squabble. Time up, let's go back to our work."

The moment of laughter continued for a while among us. While walking back to work, Rahul lifts his hand and puts it on my shoulder, "Mathav, get ready and give me a call, I will pick you up in the evening."

The clouds of the afternoon passed fast. After returning from the office, I refreshed and dressed up in my favorite white-t shirt on which was printed "just do it" and blue jeans with my favorite white shoes from Nike. With my friend on one hand, I'm waiting for Rahul.

Soon after, the loud horn from outside my home reaches my ears. I run to the balcony, grabbed his attention and shouted,

"Rahul, wait for a minute, I will come down."

Then, I took my violin bag on my shoulder and jumped from every three steps. There are screams in my mind, "Today, I'm going to play my melody." *The art of excitement.*

As we reached Lahe Lahe, my colleagues were standing near the gate with hope and excitement on their faces. He slammed a break in front of the gate. The greetings begin with, "Hello guys, hello guys."

I got down from the bike. As he parked near the gate. Alex blisses, "Hey, you got your violin, amazing Mathav!" I smiled.

With her cute chirpy voice, "Rahul, see who is late today?"

Rahul turns his head around for a moment, "It's Janu's voice, where are you Janu?"

"Hey, look at me man."

"Hey sorry! Janu, where is your kit?" Rahul stifled.

"You. Insane!!" She smirks and pulls his arms to hit on his hand.

As we entered the jamming hall, the yellow lights glowing on the sides of the wall were welcoming us for the musical nights. We five took our seats near the wall. The session was about to start, as we reached 10 mins earlier. I opened my violin bag and took my bow out to start the session. Rahul asks, "What song are you going to play today?"

"Rahul, Let's go with the flow, I'm new to the place and let's see how it goes."

A quick intro started among us. I felt something new, as I didn't interact with new people earlier. After the small intro of the big crowd, the session started. One guy in front of us, starts with his melody voice,

"Oo...
Ho Ho Ho Ho Ho Ho…."
My eyes start to search his soulful heart, "Who is he?"
In the rise of love, he continues,
"Phir Se Ud Chala…."

In a quick turn, the ambience lights up and every-one's chorus starts to flow relentlessly on the floor. I read everyone's heart. *The art of music.* The platform to express our musical love, people catching up with their lyrics and the back-to-back songs emerging from all the corners of the hall. The perfect night for the musicians. Thereafter, the group of girls egged everyone on, as the event started.

Oh, God. Is this a dream? No, I pinch my forearm. The harmonic rhythm of the wave exhilarates in the group, No more searching for her. I found my girl, my love, she is in my eyes. Such a pretty woman on the floor. It feels to me like an unbelievable moment. I told all the seven wonders to be ruined, as she is the lone wonder in my universe.

The yellow lights on the side wall falling on her dancing earrings, pinky face glowing under the yellowish lights, she captures my attention with her dazzling eyes.

With a quiet face, she sits at the corner of the group. It's just opposite to us. I lost my melody for a moment apparently, as she was there. When the group pitch was getting slow, her pretty voice raises from the other corner the sound of singing reaches me,
"Tere bina beswaadi beswaadi ratiyaan, oh sajna…"
composed by A.R. Rahman.

The voice of my love seems to gleam with emotion and love. The lingering echo of the group catching her pitch, the rhythm perfectly matching our vibe, joy embraced home and blessed the space. Behind the walls, my ears focus on the warmth of her melody which is arousing and soothing my heart. *The melody of my love.*

I waited for the moment. Ya, the portion to express my love, the hidden love. My heart is urging me, "Mathav, it's your time to flower your melody." I took my bow and joined with my muse to play the scale of,

♫…..♫….. ♪…… ♫….. ♫…… ♪…..♫….. ♫

♫…… ♫……. ♫….. ♫

♫…..♫….. ♪…… ♫….. ♫…… ♪…..♫….. ♫

("The nights are tasteless and dull,
They don't pass by easily")

I played the scales of the remaining portion to elicit everyone's emotion and joy. The voice of my love adds all the elements of beauty to my music. Everyone's eyes are on me. My friend's faces are shocked without taking their heads off and thinking about, "How my hands are playing on my friend!"

After a minute of play, there is a big cheer and an applause from the crowd, "Nice bro, Nice bro!" I feel like I'm walking in the air and jumping over all the clouds.

Quickly, the session is progressing without an end. From one to another, relentless on the nights. After the two hours of our melodies, the event does not seem to have the heart to end. But we ended with a big applause for all the amazing artists. *The art of inspiration.* I feel so grateful to be a part of this amazing jamming.

Every moment is to cherish,
In the life of an artist.

The group starts to scatter too quickly. My eyes tread on her heels and her breath, she turned her face towards me, my heart pounding in the rhythm of her every step, as she is vibrantly moving close to me.

With her cute grin, she says, "Hello, I was mesmerized by your magic, it's outstanding man, keep up."

I whisper, "Thank you."

She asks, "By the way, What's your name?"

"Mathav."

"I'm Thara, Nice to meet you."

My inner child bounced back with a question, "Mathav, ask something, don't let her go quick."

I think she heard my hidden voice, "Mathav, I think I have probably seen you somewhere, do you feel the same?"

Again, my inner child asks me to say, "Mathav, tell her no!" I buried all my search for her and pretended to myself, "No, Thara."

"Not Really?" she asks again.

"Ya, I think so."

"Okay, Actually I'm a singer and I'm part of a music band and we are looking for a violinist, are you interested to join our group?"

"Sorry. As of now, I don't have any interest, don't mistake me."

"Hey, no problem Mathav. Can I have your mobile number, if you don't mind?" she asked.

I felt so happy to share my number, in search for my love I flirted, "Ya of course, here it is."

I called out my long ten-digit mobile number. She calls me back with a small amount of excitement on her face. After her anticipation, she asks,

"Mathav, ningal malayaliyaano?"

"How do you know?" I was shocked.

"It's not a big deal, your caller tune." She smiled.

"Ya, basically, I'm from Thrissur. Are you Malayali?" I asked.

"No, Actually, a girl in my music band taught me a few words. I adore the way you guys speak. In particular, I love how the slang is pronounced. It's so charming to listen to."

"It's a great honor, Thank you." I was enthralled.

With her glittering eyes, she adds, "Mathav, in the future, if you feel like joining, please let me know. You will always be welcome. You are a good violinist."

"Sure, it means a lot." I whispered.

She turns her head around for a second, "Okay, Mathav. I have to go! My friends are waiting and will catch up next time."

My longing wants her to stop, it's pleasing that the conversation is incomplete and unfinished. In reality I have nothing to lose, as I have lost my heart to her, which I waited for a long time. *My love,* "AMMU" slowly disappeared from my eyes. I felt like a part of me was missing in the air. But the cat in the corner of my house danced happily like a four-year-old baby. "I met my love." In the happiness of melodies, we left the place by picking all the energies of the music night.

Next morning, the vibration of mobile buzzes on the table, the screen lights up. I tap the notification. It's from Thara,

"Hello Mathav, shall we meet today? I will tell you more about our music bands."

I fumbled for a second, and replied,

"Hi Thara, sure"

"Where shall we meet?"

I was grinning as she sent a quick reply. I replied, "Chai days!"

The excitement pops up too fast, "Have you been there?"

"Ya, many times" I said.

"Then we will meet there, evening at 7 p.m."
"Sure, Thara."

The melodies of my universe start their butterfly dances and the whole day, my mind was running about our innocent date.
What to say?
How to dress up?
How to speak?

Lot of questions, I asked myself and answered myself. For every hour, I turn back to see the time on the big clock, but the hour hand is moving at a snail's pace. I asked him to run fast. He ticked slowly, "Mathav. Hold your horses." Moreover, I thought of giving a boost to energize his speed. "When will it be 7 p.m.?" I stare at him.

I went half an hour earlier to the shop, took a seat near the entrance and waited for a while, thinking about the musical nights and my first sight of Thara.
After thirty minutes, at the exact time, she came with the most adorable dress in this universe, my favorite pink colored top with blue jeans. As she walked towards me, I was tickled pink in the Larry.
She grins, "Hi Mathav"
"Hi," I showed my 32 white teeth.
After looking at her eyes, I forget all my preparation for the day. I stammer thinking about what to speak, then from my little mind lighted up an idea to ask like a waiter,
"What do you want to have, Thara?"
She muses, "Let's see the card."

She led me to the bill counter and after seeing the big list, "Elachi tea - regular, for you?" she asks.
I said "Ya, same."

During the time of preparation, silence travelled between us. I love every minute of silence to witness her cuteness. Her eyes twinkled, the thin layer of kajal, replicating the F-Holes of my violin, transmits the quaver and vibrates by her eye's resonance which is purely refining to my eyes and enhancing the feeling of me to express my love.

"Excuse me, your tea please" the hushed voice interrupts my crazy peeking. I picked up the two teas, the scent of cardamom wafting over me like the semitones, but other than her cool-water fragrance, there isn't much of an aroma. Then I turned back, suddenly, my hand shook as a girl stepped by, some droplets of tea splashing across and fell on Thara's hand as she was beside me. Her eyes widened and her expression twisted in a puzzlement and unease. She took a deep breath. She reflexively cradled her stinging hand in an attempt to cool the tea spill with her other hand,
The girl said, "Oh, sorry, sorry please" her voice filled with guilt and agitation. I placed those tea cups on the table which is beside me and I ran fast to the counter and grabbed some tissues to wipe it off,
"Thara, use these."
Her eyes seeking support, her heart pounding with some discomfort,
"Thara, give your hand."

As she lifts her hand, I wipe all her suffering pains and the tea stains.

Again, the girl pleads, "Really sorry!"

Thara brushes away the discomfort and shakes her head with a quiet laugh, "I'm really fine, I'm okay."

I felt a twinge of remorse in the corner of my heart. I should have carried it carefully and she is hurting, it is my fault and it hurts me too. Even though it hurts, Thara smiles reassuringly, "It's nothing."

"Thara, come take the seat," I guide her to the table beside the walking path.

"Mathav, thank you."

She was distressed. I never imagined that our first date would cause her grief, her pain reflects me that I was careless.

She listens to my pounding heart, "Mathav, cool! don't feel bad, I'm alright." Her warm chuckle restores some serenity to the situation. But whatever, my mind was running in grief and was holding on to the big anxious issue.

I nod, "Okay"

She then began to tell her tale about the music band, along with many other fascinating stories of her college time. Inclusive of, "How she got to know the band?" and "What was her progress?" and some old interesting events. I listened, just listened to all her heartful talks. Nothing to say, her music story is inspiring me and telling me that, "I have not yet done anything in this world." I didn't express anything. I kept quiet, my respect for her increased by every fraction.

The conversation of two artists,
A never-ending inspiration.

Later, she asked me, "Mathav, I love violin, tell me about your inspiring story, how you learned?"

I whisper, "It's not a big story Thara, I learned it from my mom, I love to play all alone, just to forget me and myself in this world."

She nods, "Ya, sometimes."

A fraction of silence walked between us. Then, her mobile buzzes, she taps the screen and greets, "Yes, Lipsa."

A minute later, "Mathav, my friend is calling, she is waiting for the room key, I forgot to inform her, I have to go, we'll catch up later."

I nod, "No worries" and I said "Bye"

While walking away from the table, her foot path asks me to follow my dreams, as she is my dream. I walk on the other side of her path, carrying a little anguish inside me, as my love left with the pain, which happened due to my heedless act.

No calls or messages throughout the next two days. The small fear and vulnerability in me, forces me to stay silent. While scrolling down the feeds on insta, there is a cheerful and vibrant post. Yes, Thara was embracing the pink theme and celebrating the beauty of cherry blossoms. She posted a picture of her in the pink dress hugging a cherry blossom under the tree.

All my colorful love is in the single picture, I gazed for a minute and smiled in my heart. Down to the post, she mentions a caption,

"Welcome Pinky."

Following the appearance of my favorite color in the image, I comment on the post,

"Yoo Too Pinky."

And I hushed with great excitement, "What will be her response?"

Bangalore has its own unique beauty. In April, the streets of Bangalore will be blooming with the pink cherry blossoms. Do you fall for it? If you're Bangalorean, ask yourself? And ask every inhabitant of Bangalore, everyone will fall for it without any apparent reasons. My love for the pinky wonders,

I never thought that,
I could fall for the summer.
In the shades of your presence,
Bangalore blooms.
With the color of elegance,
Bangalore shines.

In my clouds,
No other girl is beautiful,
Like you!
As much as you!
Don't fall on the roads,
Take my infinite heart,
And fill your love.

After 10 minutes, I got a notification that she reacted with the symbol of love to my comment. I smiled and relished that I had good flirting skills.

After some days, we began having frequent conversations on our phones. It's our wavelength or something. I'm not sure what to say exactly, but everything seemed to mesh well with one another. We began to talk more and more about music, then chatted about workplace rather than our personal lives. All my nights are music nights, she sings her songs. *I listened, just listened.*

One fine day of June in the office, I'm thinking deeply about correcting some syntax errors. My mobile phone rings, my pinky is calling me to fill my heart, I tapped and took the call.

"Hey Pinky," I answered.

With little excitement in her voice, "What?"

I blush, "Hey, nothing Thara. Tell me."

"I knew man." She smiles.

"Okay, okay, what's up?" I twirled the context.

She asks, "Mathav, my friend Lipsa is getting married soon, so she's planning a quick trip to Coorg before that. Next month is monsoon and the weather will be fantastic. It would be great if you could join us."

"Thara, I'm okay, but I won't feel comfortable with your friends." I replied.

"Hey, don't worry. I will be there and you may also give Rahul a call. What do you think?" She asks.

"Thara, give me some time, I will confirm with you, I will check with Rahul once."

"Mathav, the climate will be cozy, please make a plan, it'll be a wonderful memory with lots of fun," she asks wholeheartedly.

I said "Thanks Thara, for asking."

She greets, "Hey cool. Mathav."

I feel I should go with my love, just to spend every second and every minute of the day in her company. And there's a hint of excitement in my heart. We had just started to talk for the last few months and neither of us knew anything about the other. I don't know how she trusts me so fast. What made her trust me?

The story veiled in her heart,

"Is the theory of the parallel universe being true?"

God, I have to be in her place to quench it. *Trust won't be asked or begged for.* My mind pretends not to ask, but curiosity drenches and soaks me deeply. What made her trust me? I hold on to my thoughts.

In addition, nobody had ever trusted me in my life except my mother. My days are evolving, little by little, with fresh experiences looming large in my mind. "Thank you, Thara," for realizing all of my empty dreams. I owe nothing to pay off except my love. *Nothing. Nothing.*

I swear,
Monsoon is ours.

Chapter-4

Mini-Getaway

Travel is an unknown medicine for a joyous life. The next day, I pushed my pal to go on the trip. He's an exciting and laid-back man, always striking fun around him. He is the perfect companion on our trip to make it more interesting. Day by day, the excitement ruined my sleep, my heart was too thrilled waiting for the days that I would spend out on a trip with my love.

"When is July 15th?"

"How many days are ahead?" was the daily check I did with my calendar as I lay in my bed, first in the morning and the last thing in the night.

The exciting day has arrived. We planned to begin our trip from Thara's apartment. We took an auto. When we reached there, three people were waiting near the rental car for us with a big bag on the shoulder. A picture-perfect frame for the pioneers.

"Thara, he is my friend Rahul." I introduced him. "Hi, Thara" he smiles slightly.

And Thara introduces her friend Lipsa and her fiancé (Rachin). After the warm handshakes, we dumped our luggage in the car boot. We began our trip, Rachin in the driver's seat, Lipsa in front and the three of us in the back seat. The music is playing. In excitement, everyone's eyes are out of the mirror to steal all the chasing clouds. Other than the low whispers, there is not much conversation. The tune that played between us for a while is quiet. Logically, there is a shy connection.

Rahul knows me,
I know Thara,
Thara knows Lipsa,
Lipsa Knows Rachin.
The strange companionship.

Trip with strangers is definitely an adventure to embrace the diversity of life.

Soon after, Thara took a small diversion from the chasing clouds and asked, "Lipsa, when is your marriage?"

Lipsa took a glance at Rachin and she answered, "Still the discussion is going on, I hope it will be finalized by next week, Thara."

With one leg on the acceleration, one eye on the side mirror, Rachin shifts his gear, "Guys, you should plan for our wedding, mostly it will be in Mumbai."

Thara shifts her gaze on me and Rahul, she asks, "Ya, Rachin. What's special about your marriage."

"It's quite a surprise Thara, we're planning something fun to make the party more engaging, don't miss our wonderful occasion."

Thara nods, "Sounds interesting, definitely we'll be there!"

Lipsa with the stretched seat belt, turns back from the front seat with excitement in her eyes, "Thara, you know what, I can't get over how my family accepted our love. I'm still so shocked about it."

I whisper slowly, "Lipsa, you are lucky to have an amazing family, who supports and accepts all your decisions."

"That's true, Mathav."

Lipsa and Rachin, opened up on their beautiful love story and it was engaging us so pleasantly, I felt like it's not a strange trip after our heartfelt talks.

"I made a playlist for this trip," The voice of my love hushes.

"Thara then connect your mobile," Lipsa whispers and she turns bluetooth on the widescreen of the stereo. Then, we cheer among ourselves, starting with the chorus of the song. There is a flurry of happy sounds inside the car and small dances on the seats.

Almost as we were near Mysore, Thara said in a hushed voice, pressing her hands on my arm, "Rachin, stop the car. I'm feeling suffocated."

He took a glance at her face and her discomfort, "Thara, just a minute, let me find a place, please take a slow breath" and he pulled down all the windshields for the fresh air. He had his eyes on the road, searching for a safe stop.

Suddenly Lipsa shouted, "Rachin, see that wide tree, it seems like a resting place, stop there." As he stops the car, Thara pulls a door and rushes fast for the fresh air.

"Thanks guys, I need a minute." Rachin turned off the car and we all rushed out to support Thara.

Lipsa held her shoulder softly and asked "Are you okay?" Quickly she begins to puke over the ground. It was difficult to see her that way. She was not steady and was looking for supportive hands. I rushed fast and opened the car boot, brought a napkin and water.

"Thara, use this."

She groaned weekly, "I'm sorry about this."

I nod, "No, it's not a problem, just take your time."

She barely held, "Thanks guys" and she sipped the water slowly, trying to compose herself.

I ask, "Do you need any help?"

She muffles, "Thanks Mathav, it's just motion sickness, I'll be alright in a few minutes."

We sat next to her, gave her a pep talk to get over her sickness, bided our time till she felt better and then we resumed our long journey. Rahul took the front seat. Lipsa came back to make her feel comfortable. She was okay, but the fun atmosphere was interrupted and the incident ruled our playlist. She looked weak in my eyes. I worry a bit about how she is going to manage the next two days.

Suddenly, Rachin questions "What happened, Rahul? I'm noticing that you are thinking deeply, since you came front."

"Rahul, are you okay?" I asked.

There's a twinkle of mischief in his eyes and a small smile tugging at the corners of his mouth,

"Nothing Mathav, I think Rachin got ideal rest, because of Thara's motion sickness."

Thara flusters a bit and asks Rahul "What do you mean?"

"Hey cool Thara, He was driving for a long while, that's what I mean." Rahul chuckles.

"Hey you!" She laughs "ha-ha" a hoot of laughter rises against the sun. Soon after, we found a shop for our lunch and as a soothing agent, we bought a lemon and ginger for her. After lunch, Rahul came to accelerate our trip. In the hum of conversation, she put her head on Lipsa's shoulder. A slow lofi is lulling her and she napped.

The captivating rhythm of the mist, which it is known for in the monsoon, is falling on us, as we get closer to Coorg. Our eyes are drawn entirely by the lush vegetation along both sides of the road. The world transforms into an enriched beauty in the greenery. Pure affection fills the air, and the scent of coffee from the estates captures the grandeur of the land. The sunlight is being filtered by tall trees, the winding waves of mist are falling on the leaves to shimmer like the diamond and beckoning you to explore this tranquil area further.

It's evening 5 p.m. We reached our booked home stay. The excited eyes are tired from travelling the long way. We rushed to our room, its small dormitory with 5 beds, then quickly my eyes caught the doors of the balcony and exhilarated me to open it. Its peerless view showcasing *the beauty of Coorg.* The mountains are wearing their smoky dresses, hazy clouds are kissing the heads of peaks and softening the edges of the world, inviting us to dive deeper into this serene, the magical space. We refreshed slowly, had our dinner in comfort, talked and slept soon to explore the beauty of the monsoon.

On Day 2 of our trip, we intend to visit Mandalpatti. My friends are in the urge to prepare themselves for the day. I push myself in the blanket, turn my head over to the window. The droplets of mist shine in the monsoon. The soft voice of my chirpy bird falls on my ears, "Hey Mathav. Get up soon, we are almost ready for the day."

"Five more minutes, Thara" I tune in the lazybones.

Rahul yells, "If you are not getting up, we will take you to the cold-water shower."

"Hey no, no," I rushed fast to the washroom.

We had our breakfast at our homestay and started our day-2 with group selfies. Following the google maps to Mandalpatti trek point, led us to wander in the curves of empty road and the green enchantments. There are no villages and people towards the peak. At one point, Lipsa asks, "Is this road really taking us to the trek point?" No one knows, except the google map.

All of a sudden, the car jerks abruptly and the engine sputters, everyone's eyes are slumped with the abrupt shock and worry. "Rachin, what happened?" the voice quavered from the back.

"Guys, I think the front wheel struck in the watery puddle, don't worry, I will handle it," he shifts our fear to the first gear and slams his leg hard on the accelerator to roll out.

"Come on, come on… just a little farther" the voices of us accelerating the car. Again, the car jerks and the wheels dig a narrow puddle pushing us back. "Guys, let's get out and push from the backside." Rahul mutters.

When I got out on the watery road, I could see our car was inclined in a 20-degree slope for the support. We began to push out from the car boot, but the engine made strange noises and a slight splutter. Rachin slammed the hand brake and he came out to open the front bonnet. The engine merely coughed and died. The heat waves in the drizzling mist and the burning clutch smelt hard in the unwelcoming mess. Rachin yells. "Guys, we have to wait for some time, the engine got overheated."

I start to glance around the place, there are no passersby on the road and no vehicle movement. The sun rises and sets between the clouds. The loaded map showed just two kilometers ahead to the trek point and no signals to call for help. Everyone's eyes are filled with emptiness, what would be next? Thara and Lipsa on the other hand are worrying, as no one could help us and we have ended up in a strange place. Rahul is pouring water on the frustrated engine to reduce the heat.

After ten minutes, Rahul's eyes twinkle with some experience. "Rachin, I'll try once, let's see If I can get out of the pit." His voice asked us to push from the car boot. Rahul accelerated by adding the initial torque. The increased torque in the wheel gripped our strength and flushed it out from the pit.

"Great guys, Great" the voices of Lipsa and Thara, relaxes from their intense anxiety. He parks our car aside and we bide our time as the engine to reduce his anxiety.

Soon, a four-wheel powered jeep, humped up from the far and approached us. When it crossed, windows were pulled down, there were five boys in the backseat, dressed in a thin raincoat. They look excited and the laughter fills the empty road. We realized that we were on the right path to the peak. After seeing the jeep, the deep breath smudges the mystery mist. In a newfound hope, Rahul pulled the car door, "Guys get in, let's go, Mandalapatti waits for us!"

We reached the base zone. There were eight to ten jeeps standing one by one in the row, to take us to the peak. We took one rental jeep. As our vehicle started, the rain began to shower against us. The road was rugged, our vehicle danced on the rocky path and plunged into the muddy ruts. The rainwater streaming on the mud road and the returning jeeps splashing it high. As the jeep went through a series of bumps, the suspension system put forth a lot of effort to absorb the impact but we bounced around in our seats, our laughter and shouts mingling with the engine's boom.

Landscapes stretch wide and the rich flora fills the frame. Rahul took his camera to shoot all the wonders of lush greenery. The jeep ride takes us through the views of the Western Ghats valleys. In the middle of the way, the rain stops and mist reduces, Lipsa raises an eyebrow and she points, "Guys, see that mountain, It's Incredible!" Rolling hills and rich foliage blend into the far-off horizon as the scenery opens up into a broad panorama. Thara, wide eyed, exclaimed, "Worth it dude, it's amazing, even more incredible than I imagined."

The joy on our faces is uncountable. The jeep stops at the hiking point. We had to climb a bit to take in the breathless view of Mandalpatti and the driver asked us to come back in one hour. We start our last steps of hiking towards the peak, the place glances in the shadows of the evening sky. It's 1 o'clock but it seems like evening six. As we walk over the incline, we clasp our hands and my footsteps on the flat rock reminded that,

"When we are strolling hand in hand,
The climbing pole is just an attractive stick,
and The shelter is just a stone in-front of our arms."

The mist clings to our soft skin and the wet kisses contrast with the crispness of the fresh air. The mist wraps around us like a gentle embrace. She is holding my hand on my right. I take a look at her, my eyes blush. She was more adorable than ever, the mist on her hair shines in the love of my eyes,

The mesmerizing mist,
Kisses on her head,
The tiny dews,
Shining in my love.

I swear - Monsoon is ours.
And It's not a miracle,
Fall for us,
Under the pretty skies,
To grasp her hand,
More tightly than ever.

The cool mist showered continuously, one hand with the camera, Rahul recording the vlog on the trailing, "Guys, just a bit more, and we'll be at the top."

At last, we reach Mandalpatti Peak, the breeze feels refreshing, mist flows continuously against the wind, fog moving with the loop of clouds, lost in the hidden gem. I had curiosity in my mind to identify either the rain or the mist. Almost all of our dresses were wet and the view was nothing short of spectacular, covered with the fog, bringing friendship and nature into perfect harmony.

Lipsa and Thara start to run over the green lawn of the mountains. She rushed towards me and asked in joy of excitement, "Mathav, take my picture!"
She stretches her arms around herself, as I take my mobile from my pocket. The breeze softly tousled her hair and I froze the moment in my heart and in the camera.

Rahul, while recording the vlog, goes on, "This is really amazing. It is breathtaking. I see why so many people are raving about this place, "Cheers guys," he is excited over the air and pans out, showing us in silhouette against the vast landscape.

I began to shiver due to the chilly wind and the falling mist. As soon as I saw the other individuals, I realized why the majority of them were wearing raincoats. Every now and then, the mesmerizing mist is like a tiny dew on her hair, reminding me of the new life with her. My love thrives between the top of mountains and the monsoons.

When we are back in the jeep, on one hand, I'm enthralled, but on the other hand, "Is this world so beautiful?" I gaze at her.

The cute smile on her face and the twinkling glitters of her eyes, "Yes, this world is lovely."

"Thanks, Thara." I grin.

"Why? Mathav."

"Thanks for convincing me to come, this is my first and one of the best experiences in my life."

She hails by raising her cute cheeks.

Rachin in the jumping voice adds, "Lipsa, hold it hard, there is a series of bumps." In a fraction of a second, she bounced from her seat as her head hit slightly on the top and with her stammer voice she yelled, "This is what off-roading is all about, the ride is wild, but still, it's worth it."

Rahul stifles his laugh and shakes her hand, "Lipsa, you have good coping skills." She laughs.

We began to drive back to the homestay after taking in the breathtaking scenery and the thrilling ride. Still, my body shivers from the cold. My love is warm because of its purity, but it refuses to exchange the heat. I ask Rahul to turn on the air conditioning. Gradually, my shivering stopped. The car roars with laughter and cheers as it speeds down the curves. It appears as though the world is a little brighter because of the companion's enthusiasm and the joy. We reach back, it is 6.30 p.m. I took a warm bath to revive myself and we had our dinner. While returning to our dormitory,

Thara asks "Shall we do music jamming?" Rachin has doubts, "Are we? here,"

She whispers, "Yes, we can do jamming without musical instruments. I will play karaoke and see how it goes."

To make it interesting and to make the night endless, everyone is okay with her. After reaching the room, we sit around, she places her mobile in the center and she plays one by one famous songs on the karaoke.

If you are going to listen to our jamming, I would prefer, please don't, it will screech your ears/-

But actually, we forget where we are. As the music flowed from the top of the head to the bottom of the leg, for every karaoke, we matched our group voice. There are some lags in everyone's voice but the companionship drives the magic, it took away all the fatigue and the chill of the night makes it memorable.

After sometime the silent killer, Rahul points at us and asks, "Guys, we're jamming for a long while. Shall we play Truth or Dare?"

Lipsa jumps from the seat and she lifts her voice, "Guys, I'm ready."

Even thought I was too excited about the new game, she turns on the dim lights to create a warm ambience. Rachin grabs a water bottle and by holding it in the center,

"Let's see who's gonna be the first?"

Thara grins, "Let's spice this up."

Rachin spins the bottle and unfortunately lands on him, "Hey, guys I didn't spin it properly, let me do it one more time."

Quickly, Thara picks the bottle from the floor and she hides behind her, "No Rachin, you have to!"

He took a note around us, as our eyes tied his word, "Okay guys." He accepts the game.

"Truth or Dare?" Thara asks.

He nodded on Lipsa and whispered, "Truth, Truth."

Rahul jumps in excitement, "Guys, Guys I have a question"

"Okay, Go ahead."

"What's the most romantic thing you've ever done?" Rahul asks.

He thinks for a minute and glances at Lipsa, "Actually, I'm poor at writing poems but I tried and wrote a small poem about Lipsa."

"Do you have it, now?" I ask.

"No Mathav. I hope it's still safe with her."

Lipsa smiles, "Ya, it's with me, but even I don't remember those lines exactly now."

Then, Thara spins the bottle and lands on me, "Truth or Dare?" She asks.

The game jumps into my mind, I don't know what will be the question, if I tell the truth and what will it be for the dare? I don't want to take any risk. After a deep breath, I said "Truth."

Rahul knew that I'm not in any relationship, so he asked me a tricky question, "Tell us about your crush?"

With her sitting next to me, I never imagined that the question would be about my crush. I was filled with a lot of insecurities and had no preparations to escape.

How can I say this?

Then the idea finally clicked in my head, "Her name is Ammu, two years before I met her. I began losing myself to exist in her eyes. Yes guys, her eyes were home for me. We were good friends initially and I thought we needed some time to understand ourselves. But later, I realized that she was merely okay with friendship and nowhere interested. I gave up on her when she relocated to a new city a year ago. The problem is that on the final day before leaving, she revealed her plans. I lost all my hopes and it made me realize even more, how I was actually treated. So, I just moved on."

"You don't feel bad Mathav, you deserve better."

Lipsa tries to convince me.

"That's fine Lipsa, No worries." I pretend it to be like a true story of my life.

"Okay guys, let me spin."

I spin a bottle and it lands on Rahul,

I ask, "Truth or Dare?"

"Dare"

"Mathav, I'm going to ask him, I have a funny one." Rachin asks me.

He leans forward, "Call your close friend and propose."

Rahul shocks, "This is too bad guys, I can't."

Thara laughs, "You should, you don't have other options."

After noticing our intense stare, "Alright, I will dial." He picks a phone and dials the number, phone rings for a minute, we are all excited to see what's going to happen? But there is no response from the other side. Luckily, he escapes. Then Rachin spins the bottle, it slows down and pointed me,

"Oh My God, again" I shouted.

Lipsa jumps from the fairy world and asks me "Truth or Dare, Mathav?"

Last time I said truth, but this time I wanted to try dare, "Dare" I said.

She nods at me and Thara for a few seconds. Everyone's eyes are focusing on Lipsa, as to what could be her game. She grins slightly, "Mathav, kiss on Thara's hand"

Thara glances at me. I said, "No Lipsa, sorry I can't."

I'm struck by the eyes of everyone and the group screams, "Mathav, You should." Then Lipsa pulls Thara's hand, "Mathav fast, she is okay with that, Is it okay Thara?"

She grins, "I'm okay with the dare."

After a brief moment of staring at the bottle and Thara's face. I questioned him, "Can't you carry an extra newton of force to spin over me?"

He replies, "Sorry Mathav while spinning, the photons from Thara's eyes were emitted, vibrated at me and pointed at you." I was unquestionable for the moment, my voice fumbled with the racing heartbeats. She lifted her hand and our eyes started at each other, the photons interfered to produce the fairy light for our new universe. My hands shiver by the energized photons. At the speed of light, I kissed Thara's hand.

I don't know why she made me kiss Thara, I never kissed a girl except my mom in my life, "What is the reason behind this trap?" The question arises from the far behind world. But it's the sweetest dare. I kissed my love. Later on, the game turned mostly on others. Fun, laughter and happiness filled our monsoon night.

The Next day, Day-3 was nothing more interesting and adventurous like the Mandalpatti trek. The last day of our trip was spent seeing Abbey Falls and shopping around the town and we vacated our stay. Finally, we ended our evening and the exciting trip in the Namdroling monastery. With tired faces, Rahul and Rachin were driving back home, I slept for some time and lent my ears to the music by staring at the pages of my clouds.

Going on the trip will always be cherished in our life. It may be when we are 5 years old or 50 years old. The days are to remember our happy life and to tell those adventurous stories to our loved ones. *The art of living a meaningful life.*

Rachin drops all of us in front of Thara's Home. The tired bye is shared amongst all of us. We took a cab to get back from there, the memories of the mesmerizing mist and Thara's face are ruling in my playlist.

When I stepped out of the auto, every step was trembling and my legs asked, "Where are Thara's footprints?" I stare at the road for a minute but the emptiness fills in the dark lights, my bare hand yearning for her to reply. I'm unrefuted and felt the pain of missing her.

Life always gives us unexpected true friends and restores the lost hope in life. I made new good friends on this trip. Sometimes it shows you strange faces and at times lands you in good hands. *Life is unpredictable and nothing is constant.* When we have a good supportive shoulder, the days in this cosmos will never freeze, just like that my days have begun to shift.

This is the first trip of my life. I have never been to any tourist places, except for the one-day school picnic at the dam near my school. Moving on and forgetting is difficult when it's the first time in your life!

Try asking yourself about it?
The stories of firsts in your life.

Your first gift?
Your first trip?
Your first love?
And your first kiss?

Hold my hand tight,
The love and care, I craved for,
Flowering my breath,
Charming my heart.

Chapter-5

Streets of Bangalore

After our trip, she was busy with continuous concerts. During those times that I missed her, the memories with her were my only medicine to heal from the fever of her absence. The photos of her that I scroll through, fill my days. I don't want to disturb her and her passion. The messages are off for a while. Every day the sun sets at dusk and I wait for every rise, seeing the hope of my life.

A week later, it's Friday morning. The sun rises at dawn, her text buzzes on my phone, "Hey Mathav. Yesterday night, I reached Bangalore. This weekend we will go out, plan some places."

I mask my happy face in the text and pretend, "This week?"

"Yes, plan some street shopping, Mathav."

"Sure, Thara" I texted.

The excitement is over me that I'm taking my girl out. This time, it's to the streets of Bangalore. In the wide roads with her, with my crush, with my love.

Next day, I began by taking Rahul's bike to Thara's home. I call her from the gate, she picks the phone and answers in her melodious voice, "Just five minutes Mathav, I will come down."

Like the hero of a movie, I lean over the bike, stand to the side and I wait for my angel. In the meantime, my hand tugs my hair and my smile is seen in the bike mirror. Then my head tilted over the entrance of her apartment and asked those three hundred seconds to skip from this earth.

As the clock ticks, my pretty love in a short white kurti and blue denim steps out from the gate. As she approaches me, her soft sole on this earth feathers my little heart.
"Mathav, where are we going?"
"Church Street"
She grins, "Okay."

I steady the bike. She steps back by holding my shoulder and carefully sits on the back seat, "Mathav, let's go." The voice hushed the accelerator and I shifted gears for the thrilling day. The roads of Bangalore take us on a long ride to reach Church Street. I thank Bangalore traffic.

I park my bike in the parking lot and we enter into the shopping street, the roads are filled with the bevy of adults. Small shops are up in rows on the pavement. The place is magically inhabited by writers, photographers and plenty of artists. We cross shop by shop as she walks beside me.
"Hey, earrings." She points to the woman under the shadow of the tree who is selling a lot of beautiful and vibrant collections of earrings. We took a step over there

and I said, "Thara, check which suits you?" The variety of collections are placed in a row and it's sparkling in the daylight. Her eyes are thrilled at the series of collections on the display stands. I stood beside her and watched her excitement and happy face. She picks up a pair of Huggie earrings from the row and she asks me, "I like these, but I don't think it suits me?"

"Thara, just try them. Let's see how it looks."

She picks a mirror nearby and holds it close to her ear and stares for a minute, "No Mathav, I don't think so." She keeps those pairs on the same row with a confused state of mind.

"Mathav, I'm confused, suggest something which suits me?" Then, I look around the stand, my finger pointing at the pair of silver oxidized Pallav Jhumki with the white pearl. "Thara, why don't you try these Jhumkis?"

She picks up that pair, "Hey, it's really beautiful," her voice beams in enthusiasm.

"Ya, it suits you." I smile by offering a suggestion.

"Mathav, hold this mirror" I grabbed it from her. Then she picked both Jhumkis with her hands. My eyes widened as she held them close to her ear. Except Thara's face and the earrings, my eyes blurred.

"How is this?" her face lit up in excitement.

In delight I compliment her, "Thara, you're looking so pretty in these." She blushed by seeing the mirror.

"Okay, then I will take these." She told the keeper to pack the pairs.

While packing, "Thara!" I say in a rushed voice.

"What happened?"

"I have a small wish yaar, can you do that for me?" I ask. She is stunned for a minute about what I am going to ask.

"Thara, can you wear those for the remaining of the day? I wanted to see them in your ears."

After seeing those beautiful vibrant earrings, I don't want to see them just in the closed cover. Her cheek flushes in the color of pink, "Sure, just a minute."

Quickly, she takes off her gold earrings and puts on a new pair of Jhumkis. In between the seconds of makeover, I ask my eyes,

"How beautiful is she?"

My eyes blink to reply as she has already stolen my eyes. I just realized the creation of it was to see her grace. Her warm grace. And the real beauty for the Jhumki is, when it dances on Thara's ear.

"Mathav, how is it?"

"Thara, you look amazing, they're flawless."

Her smile twinkled and she grinned, "Thank you."

As we walk on the pavement, my eyes are merely on Thara's ear. On each step, my heart dangles with her earrings. Each swing from my muse paints a beautiful art of my love. I followed her, by the force of gravity from her earrings.

10 meters away, there is a tall guy with a big bag on his shoulder, taking photos of two cute girls with a polaroid camera. I like to save the moment of the day. I asked her, "Thara, shall we take a picture in this polaroid camera?"

"Hey, of course why are you asking me? Just pull me between the frames," She grins from ear to ear.

I asked him to take two pictures, one for me and the other for her. We are ready for the frames and I'm struggling for a second to pose with the ideal stance with her. Quickly, she raises her supporting arm to put on my shoulder and I place mine on hers. As we both share our shoulders, then by tagging our faces on each other with a broad smile, we frame our perfect picture. He clicked another one with the same pose.

After collecting our pictures, she couldn't help but exclaim, "Hey, this is so cute, I will keep this safe."

By looking at our happy pic, she resumes her walk. By seeing the dances of her earrings, I resume mine. As soon as we reach the Museum Road junction, she asks, "Mathav, shall we sit for some time?"

I nod.

We sat near the sidewalk. We took a minute of silence to watch around the place. Except for the formal talk, there was nothing, I wanted to do something more engaging,

I ask her, "Shall we listen to some music?"

"Ya, play some music?"

I took my earphone from my pocket, one on her ear and the other on me, "What do you like to hear?"

"Mathav, just play your favorite music!" she grins.

I scrolled through my complete playlist for a minute, "What will make her more interested in listening?" I asked myself, finally my eyes clicked 'Arms by Christina Perri'.

"Thara, listen to this!" The song takes us through the lyrics. On each line, my longing proposes to her, "Thara, put your arms around me." my eyes convey silently between the music. I know she can understand my love; I made an effort to convey it at every chance. But still, she didn't ask me if I felt anything for her though. As the music ended, I knew she wasn't surprised.

"Thara, now it's your choice, tell me your favorite music?" I asked her.

"Umm, play *Birds of feather by Billie Eilish*." I played it, as music flowed, my eyes started to stare at the pages of my clouds, roving on her unvoiced words.
Is there the same thought running through her mind?
Does she love me?
Does she want me to stay together till her last breath?

I ask myself. Music ends and pulls me back from the deep notion, then she removes my earphone from her ear, "Mathav, I'm feeling to eat something. Shall we?" I think she lost all her energy by searching for the pair of earrings and from the long walk on the street.

"Ya, what do you want to have?" I ask.

She lifted her eyes and went on deep thinking about what to eat. She rambles, "Hah, I don't have anything in mind Mathav, you decide."

In this world, there are thousands of food items, but at that second, in front of her eyes, I'm blank. I just took a minute of my eyes around me, "The Caffeine Bar" shines in the warm light, welcoming us from the other side of the road. "Thara, coffee?" I ask.

"Sure, let's go." she grins.

As we entered the shop, the rich aroma of freshly brewed coffee was moving out from all the corners. There is a big menu stuck on the wall. I ask, "Check the menu Thara, what would you prefer?" She scales up her head over the menu,

"Today, I'm going to have whatever you order, so please."

"Are you sure?"

"Ya sure"

Then, I scan horizontally each item which is stuck on the wall.

"Cappuccino, is it okay?" I asked her again.

She nods, "Ya, fine."

We took a step from the counter, the cafe buzzed around couples and with a group of friends. There is an empty table near the glass aperture, the light from the real world casting a warm glow on the table, welcoming us to share the sip of our love. I guide her to the table, in the moment of warmth she sits opposite to me,

"OMG, you're even more pretty." I convey in my smile. In her warm glow, everything else faded away. my eyes are barely on her,

She moves her head around the shop for a minute, "Mathav, I like to ask you one thing?"

"Ya, please"

"What do you love other than the music?"

This is the most sarcastic question from her. She knows how I love music, but this was the first time, I'm thinking about what I love other than the music. Oops I can't say, I love you Thara, but what else do I love to do?

I took a moment to rewind my life and I said, "Thara, I love cooking too,"

"Is it? Really?" She was amazed. "Yes"

"Then, definitely you should cook for me?"

"Why not? We will plan one day"

"Do you have any other plans this evening?"

"No," I nod.

"If you're okay, I'll take you to my home and you can cook for me"

I squeezed my hand and gazed at her for a second, "I'm okay, if you are fine."

"Excuse me," the voice sputters on us and he keeps our cappuccino on the table, I thank him. It brews with the heart, "Thara, have please."

She starts to sip the heart of my love by looking at me with a pleasant smile. Then I sip the warmth of her love. Me, Thara and the cappuccino, a perfect combination for the cozy afternoon. Because of the cooking plan, we didn't spend much time in the café, so we quickly left our table after sipping our heart of love.

As we come out from the café, the cars and bikes rushed fast. She is standing in front of me anxious to cross the road. I took a step to give her confidence. But quickly she grabbed my hand and I held on tightly for her support. Her warm fingers firmly closed around my hand, my heart pounds and races up in her warm touch.

The profound cells in my hand cries,
The bond of sweat impedes slowly,
The soft skin feathers my heart,
The sound of the beat paints my art.

Thara, please...

Hold my hand tight,
The love and care, I craved for,
Flowering my breath,
Charming my heart.

In the bounded emotions,
The touch renews my destiny.

In the melody of love,
Our hands swirls to and fro,
And, the joy lifts my toe.

I told myself, "Mathav, don't let go of her hand for all eternity." Thara, you are my destiny, my girl and gonna be my love forever. This minute I'm happy, then the reality of the next minute strikes my mind and the other side of my world stops me, "No Mathav, what if she refuses?"

"Mathav?"

"Mathav?"

The voice wakes me from the deep love and I don't feel like crossing the road. While holding her hand, I am lost and blindly walk to the parking zone.

She let go of her hand. The tides of our sea settled on the shore. We took our bike and reached her apartment.

While ascending the stairs to her home, "Mathav, the stuff in my home won't be arranged well, please adjust."

"Hey, no problem, It's fine however."

As soon as I walk into her home, my attention is drawn to the large photograph of hers clutching a mike on the stage, hanging in the hallway. Then the money plants on the corner of windows, fairy lights are hung on the window screens and the speakers are installed across the corners of the room, soothing the cozy space. It made me think that she was unaware of a boy's room.

With enthusiasm in her eyes, she guided me to her kitchen, "Here is the kitchen Mathav, what are you planning to prepare?"

I said, "Let me check, what do you have in the kitchen." She stands next to me. I opened the refrigerator and there were no vegetables except carrots and green leaves.

She mutters, "Sorry, nothing is there, we didn't bring the vegetables as Lipsa left the day before yesterday for her marriage work."

I said, "Cool, no need to worry. I got all the recipe to cook a dish, you sit and watch some movie. I will cook something special for you."

She smiles slightly and nods, "Okay, I'll wait!"

As she left the kitchen, I collected all the ingredients near the stove and started to chop off. After 5 minutes, the voice of Thara rings from the hall,

"Mathav, what are you roasting with ghee? Do you want any help?"

"Thara, No... you just continue watching movie."

After roasting the cashews in the ghee, I start to boil the main ingredient. In the meantime, I took a step back to peek at her. She leans on her sofa, by holding a foamy cushion cover. She captures my step, "Tell me what you're cooking or else I will come over there!"

"Hey, almost done yaar, 2 minutes, it will be ready." When her wait is finally over, I pour it in two cups, garnished with raisins and roasted cashews. I carried those in my hands and walked towards her.

She is excited over the moon, her face filled with the warm glow.

"Thara, here is my sweet."

"Hah, CARROT HALWA!!" her sweet voice rushes my ear, her eyes widened to accept my surprise. "It looks amazing, smells great, Mathav," she gleamed. Seeing her cute expression of excitement, I blush, "Thank you."

Then, she lifts a spoon with her soft hands and she places a piece of sweet in her mouth. Frame by frame, my eyes captured her beauty. She rolls her tongue and chews bite by bite. Half way munching, she exclaims,

"Umm, Wow! Halwa is extraordinary Mathav, Lovely! Lovely Man!"

She is excited with the taste and after swallowing the first bite, "And Mathav, I never had a carrot Halwa this delicious."

I pulled her mouth, "Do you know, I'm a Master Chef?"

She smirks, "Umm, Umm."

"Relax, cool" I nod proudly.

"I never thought that you'll cook so deliciously and the taste blends in my taste buds, Mathav."

I smile widely by saying, "That's, The art of culinary, Thara."

"You!!"

A big smile between us, cherishes the art of tasting the sweet. Each bite of the sweet witnesses the connection of our love. We are done with eating the luscious carrot halwa and watched the complete movie, it's almost evening,

"Thara, I wish to leave now!"

She whispers, "Hmm, okay Mathav."

I smile by conveying my love. Standing up from the sofa, we both move towards the door. My mind ruins me, "Why did you say that I should leave?"

I just turn back to say 'bye', the second moves extremely slowly. "Thara, Bye,"

"Bye Mathav and text me once you reach!" her voice glitches in the low tone.

"Sure, Bye."

As I took a step towards the outside, "Mathav, just a minute!" She approaches me, not like before. Her eyes spoke with care and the shadow with love,

"Mathav, Hug?" she asks me with an angelic smile. I grin and stretch my arms,

The diverse world of this universe,
Collides in the silence of melody.

The breath between us,
Travels by the empty words.

The warm embrace of hers,
Ties strongest bond by our arms.

And the two hearts pound,
In the same melodic rhythm.

The evening wraps in the soft hug.
And, her soul touches my heart,
Wipes out my fear and solace.

I don't have any words, as she shows her affection by hugging me. Yes, she likes me, but as a friend? I was unsure about this culture.

I grin "Okay. Bye Thara."

She whispers, "Bye."

I tried to say, "Bye."

The soft hug reminds me that she changed my life and how, I asked God for this blessing. The change in myself feels like I was newly born into this world. She broke all my loneliness. Now there was a change in my gait, communication and fearlessness to face this world. "Thara, you're my eternal beauty," I whispered to my heart.

"Accepting the unexpected life is totally different"

I called her, "Hello, Thara. I reached home." "Cool." The melody of her echoed around the wall. I hoped she would be lying on the bed.

"Mathav, I want to tell you one thing!"

"Yes, Thara. Do you want any other sweets?"

"Hey no, Thanks for making my day too good."

The words reminded me of the entire day and I said, "I'm pleased Thara."

"Mathav. Then?" She asks.

"The day was really good, even I loved it." I gave her a love message.

"Then?" she asks.

"Then?" I asked.

"Okay, then?" she asks.

"Nothing" I said.

"Then?"

The minute "then" was playing between us, I felt. Yes, she loves me. The love language between us, took us together to our universe, even though we were divided by the walls. It's okay to accept the night on the phone with her melodious voice. She loves me, what else do I want?

By saying "Good Night"
Finally, I hung up the phone.

She is here,
She is around me,
She is holding my Breath,
She is hugging with her presence.

Chapter-6

She Said "Yes"

A day later, my birthday. The greatest surprise of the day came exactly at 12 o'clock midnight, Thara called to wish and in the next minute, Rahul brought a small cake to celebrate. Then, he connected every one of my trip friends in the video call and the wishes from them showered on me. I praise God for all those good memories with my friends and ask him to provide them and me, a joyful life until my last breath. I never want to lose their bond.

And it's been a year since I saw Thara. My life changed after her lovely grace on me, of course it changed me completely. Everything tells me that,

God has all the plans for your life,
Wait, wait and wait,
You will be as happy as before.

Early morning of my birthday, the alarm woke me up. But still, I snuggled under the blanket, thinking about the night's wishes. Quickly, my phone buzzes with the message. I tap it, it's from Thara, "Mathav, do you have any plans for the evening?"

I text her, "No, Thara."

"Then, I'm planning a small dinner with my friends at home, definitely you should come."

"Ya, sure," I reply with the happy smile emoji.

I'm not very excited because it's just a dinner party. But my inner child is so happy that I'm going to spend some quality time with her on my birthday. Evening I left the office with a tired face. I rang the calling bell, half a minute later, she opened the door. She seemed shocked to see me. I was mesmerized by her pretty appearance. She is wearing a red ethnic empire midi dress with a long sleeve. I simply made a note in the hallway that nobody had shown up for dinner.

"Thara, are we going out for dinner? Where are your friends?" I ask.

"Yes, there is a small change in the plan, we are going out. Mathav, I brought you a new dress, it's in Lipsa's room, go and fresh up, we will go out!!"

At that moment, I was little surprised by her plan. I just gave her a tired smile and I nodded, "Okay." She shoves me from behind, "Fast, Fast…."

I went inside Lipsa's room. On the bed, there is a new red shirt and a black pant which is folded inside the dress cover. I went inside the wash room and took a deep shower and refreshed myself for the exciting dinner. I came out from Lipsa's room, Thara is standing with a black handkerchief. Her face is mixed with disarray.

"Mathav Sorry, I lied about going out for the dinner,"

Once again, the level of astonishment in my heart and excitement increased. I ask, "Then, What Thara?"
"I have a surprise for you."
"Is it?" My voice quickly turned to excitement.
"Before that I wanted to tie this hanky"
I said "Hmm. Okay…"

Then, by blindfolding my eyes, she hauls my hand with her. Every step was dark and mystery ruled my heart. I'm excited like a 13-year boy who waited for his cherries.
"Mathav, one second." She removes the blind fold, the room was pitch dark, I can't see even my Thara.

She counts in her melody voice,
"Mathav, 3…2. 1…"

"Happy birthday Mathav." Her cute surprise and joy brought colors to the room. The warm yellow light lit my eyes. The red balloons are stuck on the walls and fairy lights are hanging over the windows for an intimate atmosphere. I can't get out from the pleasant shock, but still there is an uncovered surprise on the table.

"Mathav, cut the cake!" She gave me a small knife to cut it. As I waddle slowly near to the cake. For a minute, my heart stops its rhythmic pounding, my legs start to wince and my muscles falter. I drop the knife from my shivering hand,

"Will You Marry Me?"

It's written on the cake and I turned towards Thara's face, the tears of love shed from my eyes. I can't believe the reality of my life and I ask her,

"Really?"

She ran and hugged me with pouring love in her eyes. "Mathav, I know you do like me. I gave all chances for you to tell me about your love but I'm not sure why you didn't say it? I don't want to stay just as a friend, it's deceiving myself that I'll be untruthful to you."

A fraction of silence plays between us. I can hear all her melodies but her surprise struck my mind. Now, my love is pounding beneath my arms and pats against my heart.

"Mathav, I want to be your adorable melody. Will you marry me? I will hold you in one hand and your strings of love in the other hand" she proposes to me by gesturing to my love.

I had no answer. I cry, cry and cry deep from my inner heart. She lifts her head and glances me,

"Mathav.... Mathav "

"What happened? Are you okay?"

My words stammered by her love. All my groans flittered in the seconds of her hug. She took me to the corner of the bed and wiped my tears of pain.

"Mathav. Sit, relax, and take your time."

A minute later, "Thara, it's been a year, 365 days, 12 months and 54 weeks, since the day I saw you, your presence healed my pain. My life changed far better from my gloomy skies. I have a long story, Thara, that can't be healed by anyone but every minute with you reminds me of reason for my birth."

"Maybe I can't, but I will always be there for you, Mathav," again she dabs my streaming tears.

"Love you, Ammu!!"
"Hey, I'm not Ammu?"
"My first crush." I grin.
"You said that day, Is that really me?"
"Umm." I smile.
"Uff, You crazy, Mathav."

The laughter fills the meaning of our love and the new happiness streams between us to hug blindly. Ya, I hug blindly in her arms under her warm shoulder. The moment later, "Come let's have dinner" she guides me to the planned dinner but now it's the first dinner of our new life. We left to the dining hall where we had this complete night to paint ourselves.

She arranged a candlelight dinner. Three candles on the table and surrounded by red rose petals. Smooth vegetable skewer as an appetizer, mushroom soup, and roti as main course with paneer curry. And finally, the cheesecake as a dessert. She serves her love to my plate and we start our first dinner night.

"Mathav, do you know? When I saw you for the first time in the chai days, I knew that you were seeing me blindly. Even I peeked at you, when you were off." Her face gleams in the warm light.

I gaze at her and squint my eyes and say "Hey you!"

She chuckles, as we loved our presence at first sight. "Mathav, the next day I came to see you but you weren't there, so I left early. After that, I moved to Pune and spent a few months doing concerts there. But I never thought that we will meet again and we'll be in love and you will be my better half."

"Actually, my eyes were searching for you from the next day"

"Is it?" She was surprised by my words.

"Ya" I nodded.

After dinner she gifts me a watch, The Sound Brenner Core, a smart watch for the violinists. I accept to communicate my love with every metronome click. Quickly, nature brought us a real surprise. There were thunderstorms, windows rattled in the wind and the heavy rain started outside. In Bangalore, it's difficult to figure out when it will rain. Unpredictable weather, but it's romantic weather.

"Thara, shall we dance in the rain?"

"It seems like it's raining heavily, I can't"

"Please Thara, please," my voice barely above the rain sounds. After her deep consideration, she agrees,
"Okay..."

I gave my hands a gentle tug, grip her hand firmly and stomped fast to the roof. We both are standing just a step before the wide sky appears. She whispers, "Mathav, it's raining heavily."

Then, I step under the sky where our love is showering. I stretch my arms out in the rain and wrap myself. Every drop of the rain, unwinding my heart. But she stands under the cover and stroking her warm hands. I went close to her and tugged her hand.

"Thara, come let's dance"

Finally, she steps her leg under our showering sky and I haul her to my showers,

The love drops splints on the floor,
Sprinkles its rhythm, And
The clouds clap their hands.
In harmonic intervals,
Thunders and lightning follow their scales.

Ya, there is music in nature. We dance by holding our little hearts to each other and by holding our long hands against the rain. We dance and we dance with the art of our melody, rain falls on us and flushes away my life's hardships for the new beginnings. After 10 minutes, the rain stopped and we were back home.

Our red dresses are wet, she is so beautiful in the wet top and she grabs a towel from the table and starts to wipe and dry off my head. I ask,

"Do you love dancing in the rain?"

"Ya, but today I enjoyed it a lot"

While drying my head in silence, our eyes stare in the moody light, the rain drops from our wet clothes and falls on the floor, forming a love river to reach the ocean. The fishes are joyfully dancing between our eyes. Thara,

Take me into your eyes,
I want to live blindly,
In the color of your world,
In the corner of your home,
To waddle from one end to another,
And to have my intimate life with you.

In the melody of silence, we ramble. I reach my arm across her waist and tug her warmly. My eyes are on the tiny droplets on her pinky lips, asking me to sip slowly. Our lips are just inches apart and our eyes are drooping our lips. Our culminated lips ask the wall, 'Will you stop peeking at our romantic love?'

Suddenly the thunder strikes, the light crosses our eyes. Her hands haul my waist with her five fingers. Against this world, the warm light around us fades away to sip the tiny droplets on her pinky lips. Our peeking soft lips kiss passionately, as never before. The essence of her lips ruining me and hauling all my sense of nerves. Finally, the unstoppable kiss took us to reach the ocean bed.

To divine my love,
I dive deep into the ocean,
Our eyes are closed,
All our dresses drenched,
Our noses brush against each other,

Our lips start to sail from either end,
Our heart submerges by our hug,
Our tongue is locked by the anchor,
We know we lost our breath,
In the beautiful color of the ocean.

Still, our melody of love continues…!!!

In the foamy ocean beds,
Without the waves, we are uplifted,
I tried hard to hold the moments, but
The temperature of our cold body erects,
And we are dry by the kisses.

Our legs are crossed,
My head patted on her chest,
My arms held her soul strong,
Stronger than iconic bonds.

Finally, we sailed towards the shore,
In the tides of love.
We lost our breath, And
We lost all our innocence.

In the shore bed, she leans on me. I tuck her curly hair behind her ears. "Thara, I never thought we would start our life so early!"

"Even, I didn't think Mathav."

I smiled at her. I could hear the lost beat of my heart, flying between us under our blanket. She asks "Why do you love me?"

Thinking about it, I ask the same thing "Why do you love me?" She smiles at me.

"Love you, Ammu."

"Love you too Mathav."

And she gave her soft kisses on my cheek. The love between us promised to connect beyond our boundaries. She is my art, *My art of love.* By our discarded dresses, we spent our whole night in the shore bed with bonded hugs and tender promises. The next day,

Breezy Morning,
6 AM on her feet,
Windows are naked,
Our legs are crossed under the blankets.

Other than love, everything is priceless in this world. The sunlight glitches my eyes. She is immersed in the home of my arms. But still, I beg that the sun shouldn't rise and I ask him to fade behind the walls of the moon, because she is sleeping with the immersed beauty. The moon is slowly reducing his melody to fade away and I beg him to play for my melody, because she is sleeping in the immersed beauty.

As the kisses of flying clouds,
As the voices of the chirpy love,
As the glimpse of light from the lamp,
And as the essence of taste from the cup,
My heart of flower feathers over the sky,

Yes....

She is here,
She is around me,
She is holding my breath,
She is hugging with her presence,
Her huggy morning,
My lovely morning.

The drops of love,
Crossed my feet, and
Took away all my hopes.

Chapter-7

Where are you from?

That evening, I wanted to tell Mathav about my last night's dream which I got while sleeping on his closed arms. Life is so safe in his arms. I believe that's the true reason I got those good dreams. I called him. In the second ring, he picks up,

"Ammu…" His voice filled with promise and love. "Mathav, I forgot to tell you about my last night's dream" I remarked.

"Hahh, whether it's about our future baby?" he asks.

"Hey no, don't think so futuristic," I smirk. "Then, what was it about Ammu?"

"I was singing on the big stage for AR Rahman Sir,"

"Hahh, that's great Ammu!"

"Ya, the whole complete day I was thinking about the same"

"Don't worry, definitely you will work with him one day, I will pray for you Ammu" he said.

That minute my love for him grew, as he supported and encouraged me. My happiness overflows from the mobile and I ask him, "What is your dream?"

A fraction of silence from him, Later, "Umm, It's you Ammu."

I never expected this from him. Dreams are all about goals or achieving something which will encourage the journey of life. He is quite different, probably not quite, he is completely different. I love him, everything about him and I love him completely. I stopped myself to ask why he said that, "I'm his dream." I know I will understand this one day.

I said, "You're different Mathav."

"Might be"

His love amuses me.

If the rain from the clouds is extreme, it is said that there will be trouble, which will test life. The journey won't be constant in everyone's life, it will change one or other day in our calendar. It will change everything, I mean everything.

The next morning, I got a call from Mathav. His voice stammers and chokes, "Thara, Thara..."

First time in my life, I heard his voice, reflecting with palpable sadness and a deeply vulnerable expression from his heart. "What happened?" I asked him.

"Just now, I got a call from my home, my mom is no more."

His voice is filled with grief and deep emotions. My voice was subdued by the enormity of his loss and ceased to reply to him, "I'm leaving Bangalore" he said.

The next second, my thoughts race to how he will handle this situation? I wanted to be with him, I had to share my supporting shoulders. I have to grip his hand tightly to give him hope that I'm there. I asked him,

"How are you going?"

"By local bus, there is no train as of now. If I leave now, I will reach by evening."

In that instant, I want to share his loss to comfort him, "Mathav, right now you're not okay, at this moment I don't want to leave you alone, I will come with you. Just to help you out."

"No problem. I will handle"

"I know you can, but please listen to me, I will come, you get ready"

"Okay" he said with a shaky voice.

I packed my stuff fast to support him. I reach his home and I call him. He is stepping down, dusky face, wiping the welled-up tears. His eyes are swollen in the reddish pain of the loss of his mother. When he reached down, I just went close to him and I hugged him warmly to give him all my brave heart.

"Mathav, I'm sorry for your loss," I stood carrying a heavy heart and a speechless voice.

"Don't lose your hope, I'm here"

He cries again, he holds and draws my hands close to his heart, "Thanks, Thara" he sobs. I wiped all his shedding tears to console him and I took him to the bus stop.

We reached Madiwala and headed to a local bus. He took a seat on the window and started to stare at the clouds, the flying clouds moving one by one, his eyes waddled and my eyes were merely on him. The silence between us are the words of communication and convey my prayers. I don't have any words to console his heart,

Pain is pain,
And it's inevitable.

Soon after, I lifted his rested hands, moved it on my lap and held it strongly to comfort him, "Mathav, everything will be okay soon, if you want to cry, just cry on my shoulder, I'll be always here for you."

Then, he put his head on my shoulder and by carrying his heavy loss, we reached his native place around late evening. When we were heading towards his home, I'm not able to read it exactly because it's written in Malayalam. But there is a white board written and hung on the right side,

"Child Welfare Committee."

I recognize that it's an orphanage. I couldn't believe that his home is an orphanage. The sting of tears at the corner of my eyes welled up to spill out. The shock in my face froze me for a moment. Maybe this couldn't be a dreadful thing, if he would've told me before. *Life is unpredictable.*

I ask, "Is this your home?"

"Yes…" he said in an isolated voice.

I wanted to ask him everything which stunned my heart, but I didn't ask him anything because he was not in a position to answer and it was not a good time to ask. Moreover, the burden of his life was heavier than my fear and the shock to which I'm exposing infront.

We reached at the exact time of final rituals. The place is completely filled with a feeling of loss. The pain of missing her is rimmed in everyone's eyes, it symbolizes life and their love for his mom. He joins with the caretakers to do all the final rituals. I stood near the corner watching everything.

Soon after, her body is taken to the graveyard. The small children and the elders are staring at each other in profound emotions. Meanwhile, Mathav too ran fast inside the room and he brought his mom's violin in his hand, by holding it close to his heart. With one hand on the bow, he gathers everyone's attention with his words.

"Our mom is still here, she is living with us, we should be bold enough to accept this and to honour her by following what she says and does." He voices it over everyone.

Then he starts to play her violin, the last note of music for her, the music is something which will take us deeply to remember all the memories of the person. He does, to remind everyone about her life. As the melody began, it brought warmth and energized the space around. Moreover, he reminds everyone of her words and makes her presence felt. He came out to heal everyone's pain and all the emotions of grief, when words are inadequate.

I want to thank him on behalf of everyone, he has grown up well in this world. A perfect gentleman. I understand how he was raised by his mom. All her character is reflecting on him. I prayed and thanked his mom,

"Mom, you gave a good-hearted man to this world, thank you so much. I will take care of your son." And I thanked my God for leading me to him among the millions of people around in this world. My eyes are almost welled up by his music, reflecting it on him silently "Mathav, I'm always here for you…" the profound emotions in my heart seeping out at the corners of my eyes.

At the end of the music, he brought the word of hope to everyone's heart. In the deep absence of his mom, we all sat for our dinner. Then, the prayer is all about his mom, everyone thanked her and prayed for her. I served food to everyone, in absence of his mom. *The art of healing.*

After our dinner, everyone in the home scattered around. I went near his mom's photo with Mary, a caretaker in his home, which was placed in the center of the hall. She was telling about his mom's life story. Suddenly, "Thara, Thara," his voice made me turn around, as he approaches me,

"Thara, Thanks for coming a long way to give your support. I will stay here for another two days. Tell me, if you have to go, I will arrange your travel."

"Mathav, I like to stay here. It's alright if I accompany you while you move from here."

He said faintly, "Okay, if you are fine."

Then, we stayed there for the next two days. I spent a valuable time at the orphanage. I'm sorry, Mathav's home and now it's my home. Every one of his family is good hearted and supports each other. There is grief in everyone's heart, but their love is unpayable. I never thought about a person's life in the welfare home. But in the three days, I crossed all the paths of their life which made me understand the reality.

Everyone has a problem, but we are deceiving ourselves that it's only for me. The reality hurts, but that is true. The other side of the mirror is unknown to the world.

By the end of the third day, late evening we are ready with our bags to leave the home. All the elders of our family are standing out to show their gratitude. Mary came forward, "Thara, you are like my girl, take care of Mathav, He doesn't know about this world, he trusts everyone easily."

"Mom, don't worry, I'll take care and while coming next time, we'll get you some good news."

Taking a deep breath, she steps back and she raises her hand on us, "Jesus, bless my children."

She prays from the bottom of her heart. I gaze at her. The shared moments of these days are flooding in my mind. I took a glance at everyone and said, "Bye."

He smiles through his pain and says, "Bye" to all our relatives. With one final look back at the home that shaped him, we stepped out. We took a sleeper bus, while coming back to Bangalore. I didn't ask him anything, his pain has not healed completely. I know for the next few days he needs some good distractions. I start to scroll through all the late messages on my phone by leaning near to the window seat.

An hour later he questioned, "Thara, why are you not asking me anything about my family? I never told you anything and you didn't ask me anything."

"See, I love you as you are now. I don't have any reasons that can explain my love, Mathav all I want is you and your innocent heart."

"Ammu, Sorry. Really sorry." He grabbed my hand and held it for his support.

"Fine, don't worry." I comfort him.

He opens his heart, "Ammu. It's not like I have to hide, I never wanted to tell anyone that I'm an orphan. I don't want any relationship by sympathy. Almost half of my life is ruined by the surroundings. I didn't get an exact situation to share with you, moreover I thought you would understand one day but the day came so early. Thara, I wanted to live my life as a normal person, like you and Rahul, and most of the people here."

My eyes were fixed on him for a few seconds; my respect for him is increasing day by day and love for him growing, leaving behind this world. I close his chin with my two hands, lift his face straight to my eyes and I tell him,

"Mathav, I'm not telling this just for the moment, the real dimension of my love is you and I'm here. Now, we are normal, we are the normal people in this world, we can live like everyone else in this world."

"Ammu, I love you."

In speechless, I kissed his hand.

A minute later. He says bitterly, "Thara, the hard stories of my life are unsaid and no one knows about it, I have a long story but it's hard to listen."

Love is all about sharing the pains and all the emotions, I want to listen to all the ups and downs of his life. I can't change his past life, but I want to give my world which shows him only happiness.

"Mathav, I'm born to listen to your words, if you want to say anything, tell me, I will listen." Then, he patted his head on my shoulder, under the dark shadows, he started his hard part of the story.

Thara…

Where are you from? The only question which I failed to answer, in front of all and everywhere.

I don't know where I came from. Who are my parents? Why did they leave me alone? My days are rolled by the book without any chapters and without any stories.

Sun rises and sets,
Withered flowers in my heart,
Crying of the misery days.

No Shines,
No Blooms.

Then, I got to know my name "Mathav" from everyone's love in a small orphanage. Until my schooling, I stayed at the home, where everyone was asked the same question "Where are you from?" In that serene environment, I was raised by the lovely care-taker, Padma. Her grin brought brightness over the place, her charm was everyone's wealth. She is my mother, my father and my first love and my entire world.

In the Garden with thousands of flowers,
She was unique.

The roots are tapping like her thoughts,
The drops on petals glitter like her noun,
The stems are intense like her words,
The color of her presence will bring smiles.
And the shadow on the field,
Is for all the tiny grasses,
Happiness was around me!!

Sometimes, I feel like it's difficult to raise an own child with all the abilities and qualities from their parents. In that way, I never felt empty and handless.

She witnessed,
My heart was over the moon.
Petals started its fragrance,
Filaments dancing over the sky,
The bond of sepals,
Held against all the winds.

After my studies and college life, I moved to Bangalore. Everything was new to me, life, food and the people. The life of people reminds me to crave for care and love. Despite my courage which I learned from my mom, in the lack of belongings, there is a vulnerability at the corner of my home, it reminds me to fish about my early chapters. All those thoughts made me stand out of the crowd and stay in the corner of my room.

Then, you and Rahul came into my life. Everything changed, my life is completely new. Love and care were showered on me and I got a good circle to lead a happy life. For all of time,

For no reason,
Love endured, and
Seasons last.

The drops of love,
Crossed my feet, and
Took away all my hopes.

My heart couldn't bear the pain,
And again,

Sun rises and sets,
Withered flowers in my heart,
Crying of the misery days.

"Mom, where are you...?"

Thickness of the air is more and more,
As we are soaring over the sky,
We are in the same world,
And we are breathing the same beat.

Chapter-8

Soaring over the sky

The days are going by, but I couldn't see him the way I used to. His absence from this place indicates that he is isolating himself from everyone and pondering about something. I asked Rahul, he mentioned that even at the office, he was not so attentive and was unable to concentrate much on his work.

When I call, he sounds absent minded and his responses would be okay and hmm. It brings to my mind how much he loved his mother despite the fact that she was not his biological mother.

It's just two days to go for Lipsa's marriage. Initially we thought all of us would go by train. Later on, because of his situation. I informed Lipsa that we were not sure about attending her marriage and Rahul too had left the city for some emergency. But the circumstances demanded that I have to take Mathav out from his gloomy world. I wanted him to understand the reality and move on. Pondering on his past life would not give him any peace from his current life, it would ultimately affect his surroundings. Moreover, I wanted him back as my Mathav.

I decided and booked a flight for us, without asking him. And I called him. In the fourth ring he picks my call,

"Hello, Thara."

"Mathav, we are going to Lipsa's marriage, the day after tomorrow. I booked tickets."

"You carry on. Thara, but I'm not coming"

"Mathav please, how long will you be thinking about your mother? If she was here, even she would not have liked to see you like this"

"Maybe, but I'm not coming, Thara."

"Mathav, for me, please, please. I want to see you as you were before." I pleaded with him.

A minute of silence from him ruins me, fearing that he would not come but he said,

"Okay"

The excitement gets me, 'Hey, we are going', then I said, "Mathav, get ready tomorrow, we are going to purchase a new dress for you."

The next day, I got my periods, had bad stomach cramps. It was difficult for me to move out of the bed. I rolled under my blanket for a day and thought about him. But I wanted to get out to purchase a dress for him. Then, in the late evening I pushed myself from the strain zone. I freshened up and took him to the 100 ft road Indiranagar.

We walked hand in hand to the garment store and quickly finished our purchase. I never imagined that we would complete it soon. I had my old saree for the function, so we bought only a kurta for him. After coming out from the shop, he held my hand in the warm evening light of the streets and the pain was softening. The short walk with him stopped me from thinking of my cramps.

We arrived at airport. Everything went according to the plan except his excitement. His face was thrilled about the flight journey, I could see how he was before and I felt happy to see a smile on his face, a cute dimple on his cheeks and the rise of hope in his walk. After seeing him, I was as happy as before. Every announcement beeps and exhilarates our heart. The shuttle bus took us a long to reach our flight. His mesmerizing eyes widened over the transparent window on seeing the long runway.

The shuttle bus dropped us near our flight, the powered off engines on the two wings were pulling the thrust energy to fly and we boarded to our cabin. As we entered, the pretty air hostess welcomed us with a big smile. He settled near the window seat and dragged the seat belt around him. Air hostesses were rushing around to make everything ready to fly.

In the meantime, I ask him, "What a sudden change Mathav, I can't believe my eyes"

He said, hiding his adorable smile, "Nothing Ammu, Everything for you."

"Ammu, do you know? This is my first flight experience. Thanks for taking me."

I grinned and felt delighted because of his happiness. It shows that he is still a child at heart, his childishness jumping out and dancing in the cabin.

Every takeoff in this world will be filled with prayers. Today, my prayers are all about Mathav, "God, give all my happiness to him and give all his pain to me, I want to see him happy forever."

The engine is ready to roar by spinning its initial thrust. At the beginning of the vibration, he grasps my hand tightly. His happiness and excitement touched my heart. As the flight lifts off, his eyes are turned out for some time, watching the wide landscapes and mountain peaks as a feeling of a dream and liberty. His head is glued to the window. As seen by his innocent heart, the outside world started to fade from us and the grief of his heavy heart fell outside the window.

Our love is soaring over the sky,
By holding thousands of dreams.
Beyond, all the mountains and clouds.

Thickness of the air is more and more
As we are soaring over the sky,
We are in the same world,
And we are breathing the same breath.

I start to watch with him, all the pages of his clouds. That it's touching us, leaving us and following us. This world is so beautiful to see with him. After some time, I felt tired and sleepy. I rested my head on his shoulder and took a deep rest on my 2nd day of periods.

We reached Mumbai around 2 p.m. We took a cab and headed to the hotel where the engagement party was arranged. The function is planned in the evening from 7.30 p.m. We had enough time to get ready. My tired body pulls me to take some rest on the bed.

While I was napping, "Ammu, wake up soon we don't have time," his voice hauls me from my sleep. He is ready with his elegant white kurta and white pants. To my tired eyes, he is a picture of elegance personified. The broad and fit shoulder shows his confidence, the flash of smile bashed on his face makes him look like a new groom who is ready for his marriage. But I lay on the bed, pitched slowly to remove my blanket,

"Mathav, you look handsome man."

"Thank you, Ammu," He blushed like a ten-year kid as Mary told me and I took my towel to the shower.

When I get out of the quick shower, he is scrolling his mobile on the balcony. He is so busy that he didn't notice me when I came out. I wrap myself in the white towel and with the shapewear. After drying out my wet and messy hair, I began to wear the elegant light brown blouse pinned with the floral vines. I planned the sandal jacquard Kancheepuram wedding silk saree, contrast floral vine Zari border and the pallu of intricate designs. I hardly wear sarees, but I love wearing it as an Indian woman. It is a symbol of Indian culture and tradition. Moreover, I feel great about looking feminine.

Actually, I packed my saree with the pre–pleating, then I began to drape it over my body in front of the mirror. While draping, I felt it difficult to pin by holding the pallu,

"Mathav…Mathav…" I raise my voice.

He hurriedly walked in and lifted his head, asking, "Thara, what happened?"

"I need your help. Can you hold this pallu?"

"Why not?" he gave me a lovely smile.

As he held, I draped and tucked the pleats to my belly and I took the pallu from his hand and pinned it on my shoulder. He stands beside me watching how I'm draping my saree. With anticipation and the curiosity in his face, he asks me, "What is special about the saree? Ammu."

"Why?" I ask.

"I don't know why the saree is adding more beauty to women, I love seeing women in sarees"

I smile, "That's the power of our Indian tradition"

"Ya, but now you are adding more cuteness to yourself, this is not good, Ammu!"

"Is it?" I ask by tucking his love in the corner of my face.

"Not really," he whispers.

"I know." I chuckled.

"Can, I add some more beauty to my queen?" he asks.

"How?" he quite excites me by his love.

"Wait and see, Ammu."

Then, he corrects the pallu on my shoulders by unpinning it and he sits down at my feet and he drapes the pleats at the bottom of the saree which got jumbled. He folds it properly. By lifting his head he says, "Ammu, now see the mirror! I added extra beauty to my queen."

I was speechless. I don't know what to tell him. Who would do this for their partner? I have seen it only in the movies but never heard it from anyone. He is a gem, hard to see these days and times. I'm so happy that I have found him to cherish for the rest of my life. I'm quite lucky to receive all his love.

Then, I start to put on eyeliner, he stays behind me and stares closely at my makeover in front of the mirror. while I'm wearing my mom's golden dainty necklace. I asked him,

"Mathav, can you bring my golden anklets from the bag?"

"Ya, just a minute Ammu," he reaches to my bag and by carrying the anklets in his hand, he strolls and places his hand on my shoulder and he asks me,

"Ammu, shall I put this on your feet?"

"Really?" the pitch of my voice exhilarates, his love hiding in my eyes.

"Ya Ammu" he grins.

Then, he lifts my feet on his thigh, his soft hand strokes my light skin, he fastens the anklet around my ankle.

"Ammu, it's so beautiful on you" I glance down to my foot where it's shining with his love. Seeing his profound love, the tears from my eyes find his hand. By shifting his expression, he lifts his head up. My eyes welled up in the tears and a part of my heart stammered, "Mathav, I don't know if I deserve your love and if I'm the correct person or not?"

He stood up and held my hands on his chest, "Thara, there is nothing to talk about whether I'm deserving or you are not? We are in the real world and now we are normal people. Our relationship is something different, our silent melody is to live our dream for ever and ever. You are my dream, Ammu!"

In his speechless love, I hugged him and kissed on his forehead, then he hugged me gently by holding my waist. The love between us, reminds us of the worth of living in this world and it paints the beautiful earth alive.

In the perfect evening, the space is engaged with fairy lights and music, a magical atmosphere. As we approach the tables, kids are playing around the stage which adds a charm to the occasion. All their family members are full of happiness in their eyes. A magical Indian engagement.

Lipsa and Rachin are already welcomed on the stage. Yes, we are late to the evening. Lipsa stands in a soft sparkling bridal gown. The color of lavender makes her more pretty. Rachin in a white sherwani has everyone's attention. They both are made for each other. Looking at them sharing smiles is so delightful to watch. After a while, bowing on his knees, he holds the box to show a beautiful ring glittering in the fairy lights. Happiness is evident on Lipsa's face. She covers her mouth, surprised beyond belief and she begins to process the magical moment.

Then, she lifts him up. With the blessings of everyone, they both exchange their rings and they embrace tightly. Laughter mingles with the sign of promises.

I tug his hand closely with my hand, "Mathav, Mathav, it's so cute to see their love."
"Ya, it's too pretty Ammu." He smirks.
Then the host and the boy with the lucky draw in his hand has our attention,

"Good evening, everyone! I hope you're all having a great time. We are here to celebrate the engagement of our new couple. To embark on their journey of love and happiness and to enjoy this happy moment, I have an exciting game for tonight."

What is that game, it's clenching my mind, is there something new? I'm excited to play. She declares,

"We're having a dance challenge, the couples from each table have to draw the ticket and they should dance for a minute to the song which is written in that."

After the announcement, I was excited to dance with Mathav. The couple from the front table, went near the lucky draw and the guy pulled a ticket. Then the host read a song to the DJ, he played the song with the dynamic beat and the couple started their cute dance.

The flow continued on all the tables. Finally, it's our turn. He hesitates a little to dance in front of the big crowd, but I hauled his hands, "Mathav, this is the time to show our love, come cheer up." I dragged him to the stage and drew the ticket from the lucky draw. Then the DJ plays our song in the rhythmic and soulful beats. By grabbing his hands, gazing into eyes, we danced to the romantic rhythm.

After dancing, we took to our table to relax. An elderly lady calls me from behind, "Are you both Lipsa's friends?"

"Yes, Aunty"

"You guys danced well and the chemistry seems too natural"

"Hahh, thank you Aunty" I'm amused. She grins by showing her innocent love. Then, I turned back and looked into his eyes. His smile gave me hope. His eyes showed our future happiness. I had a question in my mind,

Was this reception ours or Lipsa's? I felt like it was ours. The magical space reminded us of our nights and brought us to the memorable occasion as it was the first time we had ever attended anything special.

Under the million stars,
The clouds gathered for us,
The moon showered the flower,
To tie the knots of hope.

Our magical engagement without changing any rings. Following the lights that flicker on the dance floor, everyone from small kids to elders gathered for the party dance. The guests on the floor created a big circle around the couple, moving around in the fullness of joy, for every step our joined hands raised up and a big smile danced with us. After some time, the DJ ends his magical beats with a power striking energy.

After our dinner and photo session, he asks me, "Ammu, shall we go out for a walk?"

"Why not!"

I left all the decisions to him. He knows me so well that no one can understand me better. A long walk by holding his arms, a safer place to live. We started our walk, after sharing some steps with him. I ask, "Mathav, I know you have a big crush on me, but you haven't expressed your love for such a long time. Why?"

"Ammu, it's just a fear in me, what if you start avoiding me after all?" He was confused by his heart.

"I gave you all the signs to show that even I love you, still why?" I asked.

"I knew that you had feelings for me, but it took me more time to understand if it's friendship or more than that."

I gaze at his eyes as we walk in silence. I recalled his calm way of handling life, reacting so fast will always end up with pain. The unbearable pain for everyone. If it's true for us, we will align anyway beyond the reasons and the struggles. He is so true to me and to my emotions. I believe that's the reason I proposed to him blindly.

Then he suddenly says, "Ammu, for a boy like me, it's really hard to find a good friend like you. For me, it's a dream Ammu and you are like my dream."

He emotionally tied my hands. If a girl receives pure love and plenty of pampering from the boy, what else will she think of? I too had the same, I need him for the rest of my life. I love You, Mathav.

To make him feel better. I said, "I believe, it's not too late, Mathav."

"Maybe, but it took me 24 years, Ammu."

The words of his longing and yearning, draw out my tears and peeled my little heart.

"I'm sorry Ammu, sorry." he said, his voice of love pampering me.

"It's fine Mathav, I'm here to listen to you." Then, he wipes my tears and tugs the swinging curly hair behind my ears.

Most of the time, we don't share our emotions completely with our partner. But, sharing a bit of emotions is like pouring water on a tree. It makes it grow bigger and stronger, to hold against all the winds, bad weather and moreover it gives the shadow of hope to everyone's life.

After a few steps, in front of the supermarket, he stops me, "Ammu, one minute. Stay here, I will come fast."

He rushes fast to the market and he comes out by hiding his hand behind.

"Ammu, I have one surprise!" His voice was full of excitement.

"What is it?"

"Guess, Ammu. Definitely you will like it"

I don't have any clue about what he brought, it's not big in his hand and moreover, he went inside the supermarket and my mind went to search in the rows of aisles, the clue clicks my mind, "Is it a greeting card?"

"No, Ammu. It's a wrong guess"

Once again, he took my excitement through all the rows of aisles, I wrinkle my eyebrow in deep thought to search beyond all the passages.

"Hey, it's very difficult to guess, show me Mathav"

"Okay" he grins.

Then, he lifts his hand from behind and reveals it to me. I think no one in this world gifted this to her partner. The gift tells me how he loves me and my emotions, the unsaid emotions.

"Biscuit" I feel thrilled. Once again, I didn't get any idea of why he is giving me a biscuit? By restoring my excitement, I told him,

"Mathav, I'm not feeling hungry"

"Hey, Ammu, I'm aware. You still don't understand why I brought this?"

"Seriously I don't have any clue"

By holding the gift, his eyes blinked, "Okay, just take a look around us, who is here?"

Finally, I felt excited and understood why he brought me the biscuits. Yes, it's quite common around everywhere, but the feeling which he gave me is ineffable to my heart.

"Are we feeding this dog?" I ask him.

"Yes, Ammu, come, come"

He held my hand to walk near the street light pole where two dogs and a small puppy are relaxing after a tiring day. The puppy with a wounded right eye, isn't aware how to lead the upcoming life. The other eye stings with the tears, I can feel the pain of the puppy which is intangible from the eyes. I reach near the pole. The pretty little face lifts up on seeing me. "We're feeling hungry" the elder dog bows too softly.

He opens the packet. I start to feed all the biscuits to the cute family. One by one, bite by bite, the puppy and their parents tasted their dinner and showered their love. Their affection for each other is evident of love and I cared for them as my family.

He knows that 'I love dogs' and he made me complete being myself and it's a great gift for me to feed all my love to the dogs.

Without any ribbon and bow, not in the big palace, without any costly diamond. He made me feel as a 'Queen', queen of his kingdom in the space of uncountable stars. Under his shadows, no matter what, he is my safe space and my lovable soul.

I stayed with her,
Held her hands,
Massaged her feet,
and Kissed on her pain.

Chapter-9

Periods Love

What's the meaning of my life? The question arises on all the pages of my clouds and now, I can shout aloud that "It's my Thara," "It's My Tharaaa." Whenever I throw a stone into the river, all I could see was the stone sinking beneath the water carrying a heavy heart. But now, her love is showing me the happiness that splits over the river. She is magic. That's the reason maybe, the lost pages in my clouds are flown easily. 'Yes, she is magic.'

After coming back from Mumbai, it's like a big gap between us, again she was busy with her concerts. But those memorable days kept me going on the new path of life, which had now merely me and my Thara. The new world is waiting for us. To cherish our love by giving birth to all the flowers in our garden. To embark on our journey by giving life to all the rivers. To celebrate our love by giving feathers to all the birds. The new world is eagerly waiting for us.

In the corporate world, I'm sure everyone will be expecting their weekends, to relax, to spend quality time with their loved ones, cleaning their homes and washing their clothes. Moreover, it's for the self-grooming and purchases too. The same thoughts crossed my mind. I was expecting. That I could spend some time with my love.

After a month, it's Friday evening. While coming out from the office, I check my mobile, and there are no messages from morning! My mind is full of her,
What is she doing?
What happened to her? And a lot!

As soon as I reach my bike parking lot. I called her.
After the third ring, she picks up,
"Hello." I observe, her voice is full of dizziness and sleepiness. "What happened, are you okay?" I asked her.
She said, "I'm okay, I felt too tired because of the late-night practice sessions with my band. I told you right, I have a concert next week."
"Ya, but still take care of your health Ammu"
"Sure. And Mathav, do you know this time? I'm going to sing a song which is composed by our band."
"Hey super Ammu, my best wishes for you."
"Ahh, thank you. Actually, I want to sing in front of you, but you said, you have an important client meeting, I'm missing your presence yaar." She drags.
"Sorry Ammu. Definitely I will plan next time"
She took a fraction of second to digest my absence, "Umm…., Mathav see, you have to listen now, I will sing for you"
If she fixes her mind, I don't know how she would energize herself, my stubborn girl. The goodness of having a persistent heart drives her to be the brave girl.

When it comes to my Ammu's melody, I will never say no. All I want is her pretty voice of melodies, which I love to listen to, even if I drive to my graveyard. It soothes my heart, brings her love and shows my shining thirty-two teeth. I love listening to her, just listening to her. She sings some part of the music. As always, she touched my heart.

"Ammu, no doubt, you will own the stage!"

"Hahh, thank you."

I smile inside my heart. But I'm reminded of her tiredness, "Ammu, I can feel, you are too tired. Soon, finish your dinner and rest. I will call you in the morning!"

She hangs up by saying, "Okay Ma, Love you."

Whenever the music plays between us, it takes all the heaviness of the head away and I feel rejuvenated. Her love for me will never fade, even if she is completely dizzy. My stubborn girl.

Then, I took my bike from the parking lot and powered my wheels. After my dinner, I walked out as usual to our preferred night date shop "Chai Days" and I bought my favorite "Elaichi Tea." I got a center table in the space, surrounded by the bevy of adolescents, where they were chewing on their weekend plans, some on serious phone calls, few engaged in silent exchanges as couples and some cute flirting too.

I pick my mobile and start to scroll through our happy pictures. The warmth of the lights is quite less today, everything around me moves very slowly, as if to ask, 'Where is your Thara?' I miss her, missed her presence. But still, we sip our favorite "Elaichi Tea" without any conversations. At that moment, I felt she is unconditionally living in me, in my happiness, in my essence, in my walk and nevertheless in my heart like my dream angel. Moreover, she is my everything.

She was my yesterday,
She is my today, and
She is my future.

Soon after, the notification pops up from her periods calendar on my mobile. As I open, 20th March is circled. I think all her dizziness is because of the previous day's strain. The only thing which rolls in my head is I wanted to stay with her to give her some pampering. Then, I left the place with full of misery but not as much of '*Queens on the Land.*'

Next day, dreaming of her pain draws me from my early sleep. The voices of her cramps haul me from my bed. The mind was completely drained by her pain. I said to myself,

"Thara, I'm here to help you recover"
"I'm here to share your pain."

Quickly, I went to the supermarket, bought dark chocolates, pineapples and a bunch of spinach leaves. Without any clue and with a big bag in one hand, I rang her door bell, the door creaked open after a minute.

The day is circled in the calendar,
Dizziness in the face,

Stains of the blood,
She is struggling to step out,
The sound of her cramps hustling my heart,
The pain in her joints breaking my heart.

Thousands of thoughts around me,
How will she handle it?
How will be the mood swings?
What could be the medicines?

In the search of the best,
Ibuprofen could be the one!
Despite the best, my heart said,
The art of my love will cure.

I stayed with her,
Held her hands,
Massaged her feet, and
Kissed on her pain.

Served my love,
In the cup of ginger tea,

Served my love,
In the leaves of spinach,

Served my love,
In the pieces of pineapples,

Served my love,
In the pieces of dark chocolates,

Served my love,
To get out from her pains,
To get out from her stains
And to roar for her passion.

The day with her, I served all my love in different forms, my only thoughts were to keep her normal, normal than before. I don't know what I'm doing, but my mad love says,

The color of red is to celebrate,
The cramps of her pelvis are restoring melodies,
The stains on her dress are beautiful paintings.

Around Afternoon, she asks me, "Shall we watch some movie?"
"What movie ammu?"
"*The fault in our stars,*"
"Okay, today it's your choice Ammu"

As we began the movie, we sat on the sofa, she put her head on my shoulder and she snuggled against my heart beat. The movie took us on a journey around the character's friendship, love and their search of life. We are near the climax scene, Hazel was reading 'Augustus last letter',

"She is so beautiful, you don't get tired of looking at her,
you never worry if she is smarter than you….."

It ceases my girl's heart, the tears from my stubborn girl's eye fluttering on love, her heart become so weak and thin to carry the words. She held my hands stronger, stronger than before. She said earlier that she never cried during the movie scene. I understood her impassiveness was just a word, to maintain her personalization. But it would come out at an unexpected moment. Where I saw that her words failed because the depth of pain is unmeasurable.

From half of the movie, there is one question which hangs on my wall of heart, which travels with me in every scene of the movie. What will be the answer from my Ammu?

After the end of the movie, "Ammu, did you notice the important driving line of the movie?"

"Ya, but do you have anything serious in mind?"

"Not too, but I'm eager to know!"

She didn't understand what I'm keen to ask her, there was plenty of mischief in her eyes.

"Okay, tell me." she said.

"What are your wishes, Ammu?"

She stares at the TV for a fraction of seconds, glazes around the walls, "Mathav, why are you thinking about my wishes?"

"I wanted to look after, if you have anything"

"It's not the right time, my love."

"Okay," I whisper.

I spent almost the entire day with her, secondly with her pain. The clock ticks, it's 5 p.m. Most of her dizziness is drowning far behind the horizon, The melody of the moon arises from the dusk.

"Ammu, shall I leave now?"

She held my hand tightly, "Really you wanted to go, you can stay here Ma."

"Ammu, I have to attend my colleague's reception."

"Mathav...Please," she drags her pleading voice.

"Ammu..."

"It's okay," she says.

But every corner of her heart asked me to stay there, however, I solely trust the moon because "The moon is ours!!" The color of purity will bring her sleep and the art of melody will cradle her heart. The strength of craters fills all her gaps. What else I wanted from the moon. Yes, the Moon is ours. I left her with the full moon and I reached my home.

Before going to bed, I tap my mobile to call her, but it is late at night, I stop myself from disturbing her sound sleep. But my heart wants to kiss her pain, again and again. So, she might feel better and rehabilitate from the pain faster and faster than anyone. I know the pain that everyone is going through for those three to four days. She made me realize without doing anything to me. Yes, she enlightens me about everything, just by her presence.

A month before, we were shopping for Lipsa's marriage. She felt lurching and tiredness in her body. I understood that she got her periods that day, she was not letting her strain out. She walked with me in all her pain and discomfort.

She stepped out only for me, the utmost concern was to dress up for me. Most of the time boys won't get pampered easily, unless it's true love. Even then, she yearned to do it for me, in all her afflictions. "That's my Thara! My brave girl."

Around 7 o'clock in the evening, we went to the shop and checked the kurta, within 5 minutes, I said "Ammu, I'm okay with this grey kurta."

She glazed the kurta in half eyes and other half eyes on the rows of collection, "Umm, it's looking good but we will check others once."

Then, I hung it on my arm, searching for my favorite white colored kurta. She waved her hand from the next row. "Mathav, this one." My love of white is on her hand, then there is no other choice.

I said "Ammu, perfect."

I tried it out, the perfect fitting on my shoulders gave me an energetic confidence. We completed our shopping in less than 20 mins. I made it too fast, just to reduce all her crampy pains.

After coming out from the shop, the lights were shining on the street, but there was less brightness in her face. I didn't understand what I had to do, I just held her hand stronger, to give all my energetic soldiers to battle her pain. After a few steps on the pavement. She asked me,

"Mathav, I'm feeling hungry. Shall we go for dinner?"

I asked, "What do you want to eat?"

"Shawarma!!!" her craving tongue pulled at her mouth to eat. Then, we went to a nearby shawarma shop and ordered 2 chicken shawarmas. The shopkeeper told us to wait for ten minutes. We came out of the shop and took a seat under the tree; my eyes were on the boy in the shop who was preparing the appetizing shawarma for us.

In the meantime, she bites my forearm to heal all her form of pain. I'm clueless and dumbstruck, why is she doing it?

I asked her, "What happened Ammu?"

"My abdomen is paining, Mathav."

I'm out of my mind, I don't know what to do!! Where to go, and got struck by anxiety listening to her voice.

Immediately, I asked her, "Shall we go to hospital?"

"Mathav, it's usual for all the women. I'll be okay. It's just the first day. That's why, the pain is more intense"

Then, I got her some water from the shop to drink, "Are you okay now?" I asked her.

"Better," she replies with her weary smile.

At that moment, I thought, I will be the happiest person in this world, even if she slaps me a thousand times with her pain. The pain in her pelvis is to share and the color of red is to celebrate. I promised myself that, till the day I die, on those circled days of every month, I would stay with her and share all of her suffering by sleeping at her feet.

The restless feet of my brother,
Lifted our wealth.
The restless sleep of my mother,
Strengthened our health.

Chapter-10

The Sudden Shock

Life is good in his arms. His care is beyond the sky and uncountable from my heart. My childish heart is jumping on its own. All miracles are mysterious. I don't have any reason why I fell in love with him, till today, I don't have an answer to everyone's question.
Why do I love him?
What will you do when you find a boy like Mathav?
I question myself?
And the answer is with my Mathav.

I will do everything. If he has no water to live, I will cut my hands to quench his thirst and I will give my soul to power his eyes. I won't say that he is good at everything, but I love his imperfections blindly. Accepting how he was, is my love. Living with all his imperfection is my love. Sharing his heavy shoulder is my love.

Next day, the sun hadn't risen completely, the gloomy clouds were moving in the silence. Around afternoon, my mobile buzzed from my sister. I tap to say, "Hello." With a stammering voice and a heavy breath, she felt hard to convey the message. I was clueless and sensed something wrong, what had happened to her?

In the stammered voice, she said,

"Didi! Our brother committed suicide!!"

My heart broke for the first time in my life, my heart was pale with profound shock, my voice trembling to accept it,

"What do you mean, what happened to him?"

"No one knows Didi," her voice fills in the mystery and the pain.

At that moment, All I wanted to do was to take care of my mom. The loss of a son is never replaceable by anyone. I told my sister, "Take care of mom, I will try to come fast."

I took a last-minute flight and left the city all alone. The pain of losing him was agonizing all the way. The intensity is deep like hammering on my head and pricking my heart. My hanky is flooded with tears. I'm completely ruined. Soon after, the memories came flooding back, as his face was appearing before my eyes,

That smiling face,
That childish face,
That courageous face,
And that caring face.

I lost my one hand and my other hand was searching for his shoulders?

"Brother, why did you leave me halfway?" "Why did you leave our mom?"

I place my head on the window seat, staring at the clouds of my other side of the world. I kept thinking about my early days, what would happen to my family? How had my brother and mother uplifted and groomed us?

My father passed away in a car accident when I was 3-year-old. My brother, my mother and a 5-month baby in her hand. I didn't know what was going on around me. From that situation our mother has been raising us. Because of societal pressure, we moved to Delhi. We started our normal life in the small village of Kusumpur Pahari.

My mother started to work as a housekeeper to feed us daily, but poverty ruined us. Initially my mom felt it was hard to provide for us with three meals a day. By understanding all our struggles, my brother stopped his schooling and started to work. As a coolie of 20 rupees daily to my home, he strengthened us in all the basic needs. To give us basic health and wealth, my mom and brother started work from morning to night. There were no lights to brighten our life, but the rise of the sun was the only hope which enlightened our small home. We don't have enough wealth, but the supporting hand of my brother and mother brought joy to our family. They are like my two hands. We felt complete. Small savings from my brother through his coolie work, we started a small food vehicle to serve all the daily workers around morning and evening in the corner of Palam Marg.

Life moved on, we were happy four on the clouds of heaven. Me and my sister started to help my mom in our weekends and free times. From the food vehicle to the small mess, our hard work paid off. Our life changed day by day, every year bringing us new happiness. We were all growing together in our strongest bond.

The restless feet of my brother,
Lifted our wealth.
The restless sleep of my mother,
Strengthened our health.

The backbone of my life,
Grown by their hard muscles.
All the veins of my life,
Stretched by their long feet.

The courage for my life,
Fed by my mom's hand.
The determination for my life,
Shared by my brother's shoulder.

My brother was like a father to me, the safest lap to sleep and share my words. We would fight for all the witless reasons, but the next second, we both would lose the battle to acquire our lovely crown and sword. I love my brother.

Me and my sister completed our schooling and I joined Bachelor of Arts (B.A.), Government College for Girls, Sector-14, Gurugram. She was interested in statistics and studied in the same college. We struggled hard for our health and wealth, but still my mom and brother never compromised on my passion. They both supported my decisions and stood with me in all their hardships.

My singing journey started from my college days. I participated in several music events, won a lot of hearts and evoked a lot of emotions. But my all-time happiness was singing to my mom. Daily after our dinner, I used to sing to help her unburden all the pain of her life and to bring a shower of happiness to my family. By hearing my song, she would take a soothing sleep for the night. That's what I loved to do.

Lipsa has been my best friend since college. I met her at one of the cultural events during my first year. I got to connect with her because she was a member of the organizing committee. Later on, she became my dearest friend. During weekends, she used to come to my home and spend some quality time with us and I used to go to her home. We shared the roads of Delhi in our friendship.

After some days, she added herself as one of our family members and she is well-aware of all my ups and downs. Moreover, she supported me financially in travelling for all the cultural events. She is my support system. Because of our friendship, I was aware of all the inter and intra college musical events. I would get to know about it from her at the earliest.

My life changing moment was during the last semester of my college days. I used to post my singing videos on social media. From that I got a lot of opportunities to sing in the official events. I started to earn on my own. During the end of my semester, one fine video of my singing went viral on social media. It was noticed by one of the famous music bands and I got an opportunity to work with them.

I asked my brother and mom, initially my mom asked me to stay with them. I knew that her fear was about how I would manage being too far away from home and not about following my passion. Later my brother convinced her. With their full- hearted support, I moved to Bangalore and started my singing.

Everything went well, but the sudden shock of my brother, I wasn't able to accept. His laughter, his support and the times we shared were screeching in my heart. He was like a brother to play with and father to guide me. By seeing the hardest page of my life from the window, I wiped my welled-up tears. By losing one hand, I don't know how I would lead my family?

The pain became more profound and hit my heart.

The anguish of loss was ruining me,

"Bhai, why did you leave us?"

By trying to bear the big loss, I reached my home. My mom sits beside my brother. He looked peaceful in the morgue freezer. After seeing me, my sister ran to me and gave me a grief hug. I wiped her tears and then tried to steady her. I took a deep breath, trying to find the strength in the dark shadows. The pain in my sister's and mom's eyes is unanswerable.

Two police, with the case file at the corner of the funeral home, was enquiring about him, "The reason for his suicide?" But at that moment, All I want is to console my mom and sister and to give them complete strength for the loss. It was already delayed because of me. After all the final rituals, my neighbors carried my brother to the graveyard. We were three women who had always stayed inside the walls.

After 23 years, the happy palace built by my brother collapsed, destroyed completely by lost hope, where every stone is layered by his love, every beam is structured by his support and every column is built by his strength. But our heavy tears, flooded all with destroyed hope.

"We miss you Bhai."

Again, I have to start from the foundation. Now it's on my shoulder, I don't know what to do?

The closed book of life, drags me to search what happened to him. No one knows about why he committed suicide. I follow his daily life to find the reasons. Every corner of the street is a dead end, No clue, No answers. Everything turned into a riddle as he doesn't have any friends to share his story. A week passed in search of the reason and his stories.

One night, suddenly the stories of my brother reminded me of Mathav's life. Both men struggled hard for their life. A meaning for their life and stories for their book. Every man has an untold story. Their past life, family situations and societal pressure. Pain has no gender, no age differences and no bar.

Pain is common,
And pain is inevitable.

The extended nights drew my sleep. The first time in my life, the fear of living ruining me, I doubted myself,
What am I going to do?
Who is my life?
Mathav or My family?
Again and again, the question of my life hangs with an unknown question.

For two weeks, almost without any conversation with my Mathav, I lost myself. That night, I took my mobile and scrolled his name, he had already sent a voice note to give me hope,
"I'm sorry Ammu, I'm here for you, stay strong."
His comforting words gave me hope and it showed me that he has had a long wait. I reply to him,
"Mathav, I'm sorry, I know you have been waiting for my message, I have lost all my hope in life. I have to stay with my mom for some days. Give me some time, I will try to solve it all."

Flushes of my love screeches.
Now, my body is just a skeleton,
Twisted and thrown off.
The life of mine sucks, Sucks hard!!

Chapter-11

The Connection of Pain

The message from Thara buzzes on my mobile, I reply, "Stay strong Ammu, all my prayers will strengthen you."

I know, the pain is inevitable and difficult to share. Her situation was different from mine. Yes, I knew all about her after coming from my native place. Lipsa called me three days before her marriage,

"Mathav, Life has to move on, accept the reality, I know it's very hard to forget. The ways in which you perceive this world are totally distinct, you received all the health and wealth from some good hearted one, but her life is different, she exists solely for you. If you're not willing to accept the reality, it will hurt both of you."

Then, she told me all about her family and how she took over all the responsibilities in her life, about her studies and my stubborn girl's passion. What I have done to her is nothing. She earns all my respect. The other side of Thara's life made me realize the real struggles. From three meals for the day, her challenges started, But the only things I faced were loneliness and invisible parents in my life. Except that, I got everything, all the wealth and the health.

The untold pain of Thara made me understand real life. That's the reason, I moved quickly from my grief and it was only for my Thara.

The same day, when Thara left Bangalore, I called Lipsa. She told me that Thara missed her brother. I prayed every day to give her all my strength. All I want is her love. I stayed quiet, waited a long time for her message. For the first time in our relationship, we got a long break, no calls and no messages for almost a month. I understood,

Pain is common
And the pain is inevitable.

Every day is again a search for my Thara, but her memories are the only essence for my life. It captivates me and drives in her absence. In a bad phase of life, staying with our loved ones will give them enough strength. But I didn't get the chance to be with my Thara. The long distance between us, made us unwind alone with the emotions and pain.

A month later, "Mathav, Tomorrow I will reach Bangalore, evening we will meet at the park." The message brought a big smile on my face, happiness lifted my spirits. Those difficult days are fading in the background. I feel like shouting out loud, "My Thara is back." Everything about my happiness is okay, but I didn't know about her, how she was mentally now? Whether she moved on or is still thinking about her brother.

In the evening, I went too early to the park. I never felt like I'm waiting when I'm looking out for her. My love is just to see her and to dwell in her eyes. In the meantime, I look around. Under the tree, there is a cute baby girl with a bubble wand in her hand. She dips it into the small bottle of soapy solution. She pulls the wand out, hauls all her breath and gently puffs, sparkling bubbles in the sunset reflecting the colors of the rainbow, she jumps with joy and chases the dreams. For her little height she misses most of them, but the profound magic of her chasing them sparkles in my eyes. Her grandpa was trying to pop up the bubbles around her, her happiness and giggles spread over the park. Her cute magical laugh floating in the air. *The art of watching* is gleeful joy. Her open heart with enjoyment pulls me to chase after them. But quickly, in between the sparkling bubbles, the steps of my love are approaching me, those sparkling bubbles gave her a warm welcome to reach my heart.

"Hi Ammu." she took a seat beside me, her face reflecting the grief and her silence walking with the pain.

"Are you okay? Your mom and sister are fine?" I asked her.

"Ya, they're somewhat good now" she replies with a sense of loss. Again, the minutes of silence crosses us, we both are watching the little heart, her focus is merely on chasing and popping bubbles out. I thought of taking my girl to the next phase of life where her dreams were still alive. I ask,

"Ammu, What's the next Plan?" "I'm not sure"

"Okay, just take some more time Ammu, I'm here"

"Hmm, Okay." There is a lot of difference in her voice, intense silence in her tone peeling my love.

"Mathav, I have to tell you something"

"Yes, Ammu"

"Please stop all your care and love Mathav, I don't want to be your Ammu."

The word from my only heart screeches into my ears, "Ammu, please don't play with me, I can't bear this"

"I'm serious. Let's break our relationship, Mathav"

"Ammu, please Ammu, don't say this again, I know you're playing with me"

"No Mathav. I'm serious, we can't carry our love to the next phase, I have lost myself"

The meaning of trust peels off and scratches my heart, blood flooded as a heavy tear in my eyes, I never imagined a situation that drifts my wind.

"Why Ammu, what's the reason?" I pleaded with her.

"Don't ask me anything, Mathav,"

Even her eyes mixed with tears coming from a pained heart. "Then why! I'm ugly, boring!!"

"No Mathav, I love you. You are most beautiful man in this world"

"Ammu, what happened, tell me the truth, will solve"

"Nothing Mathav. Please, please accept the reality"

"Ammu, I can understand your situation and since you are unstable, whatever you decide will be the wrong course of action, I'll wait, take your own time Ammu Please"

"No Mathav, I just concluded after thinking from all the perspectives, it won't work for us, please move on."

The silence between us plucks the beautiful flowers of my heart. Welled up tears in my eyes, crossed my feet and once again took away all the hope of my life.

"This is the last chapter of our love, Mathav. I know it's difficult for both of us, but try to move on. Bye."

She stands up to leave from my heart, I tug her hand, "Ammu, please don't leave me alone." I pleaded with her.

She turns her lost face on me, by wiping her shedding tears. She deserts my hand from her heart. She left the park by taking away all my dreams and all my future. Without any reason, my love endures. My empty body sticks with the pain,

Why does every pain hits me?
Why? why?

The question about my life hits hard and hard, without any reason. I plead for my love. Nothing is there in my hand to ask again and again. She broke my little heart and destroyed my paradise. For an hour, I don't feel the gravity of this world. In an allogeneic space, unorganized darkness settles in my heart. Except the word of Ammu in my mind, nothing pumps out, all my veins and arteries are blocked by her words, "Lets break our relationship." The sound of breakup is whirring around me.

With destroyed dreams, I push myself from the pain to come out from the park. The baby girl with the empty bottle and the bubble wand in her hand, is wailing loudly. Her unsaid tears mixed with my shedding pain. The chasing dreams on those bubbles, those sparkling bubbles fade by popping out its nature. Our hearts jumped with joy and chased our dreams but lost because of the empty bottle. We don't know the reason behind the emptiness. Our heart, with the same pain, stumbles on our legs on the prickle path. The pain leeches on the road. The magic of emptiness makes us thin and thin. She is magic, that's the reason I trust her blindly like a five-year kid. But the five-year kid isn't aware that all that magic is not true. Yes, she is magic.

I reach my home in the emptiness, I don't know what I'm going to do, I don't have a hope of living. I reach my bed, all my tears start to flood on my pillow, each drop stores to form an alpine glacier. The connection of pain pulls my tears,

I can't ask my eyes,
To stop crying,
They do unknowingly,

My heart overwhelmed with her love,
My brain overwhelmed with her memories.

The pain of love,
Starts to stab my heart.
I can't ask my hand,
To stop this thing,
Yes, all my stupid things.

Hard to find the reason, when
Connected by the veins,
Connected by the arteries,
And connected by the heart.

I can't ask my heart,
To stop its pounding
When she is my heart beat.

Let my eyes cry, and
My hand stab,
The connection of the pain.

I don't know why I'm living on this planet. The profound way of hiding my pain is destroying myself, but my little heart is waiting for her, longing for her in the corner of hope.

Next day, while leaving the office, there was heavy rain. My colleagues were waiting to go. I waited there for 5 minutes, but the story of the previous day flushed my tears. At that moment, I begged myself to control my emotions, but I'm unable to do so and instead I jumped into the rain, to hide it from everyone and to show myself as strong. But really, I'm not. By carrying a heavy heart on my bike, I powered my bike in the rain and left the office thinking the same, again and again. As I ride in the heavy rain, there is a thunderstorm, lightning is crossing my eyes. The drops of rain are sprinkling on my helmet, the wind is crossing and pushing me back to fall, I lose myself in her memories.

I ask the rain, "You sprinkled your melody to dance with my love, Did I play a wrong note?"
"Are there any mistakes in the scales of my character?"
"Are my melodies boring?"
"Rain, my love is pure like you!" I cry.

Rain,
Take my tears,
And hide with you,
I need to cry,
More and more,
Louder and louder,

By drenching
Under your Arm,

By holding
All alone on your feet.

But the rain shows me only the silence!!
The God too disappeared in the cloud's arms.

If she was here, I could have stopped myself. Of course, at this moment no one is there for me. Suddenly, I see a couple and their child standing under the tree, to get away from the rain. My head turns towards them unknowingly, the couple open out their hands like umbrellas on the child to protect every drop falling from the tree. It's enchanting to my painful eyes. The family is cute like them, in their world.

"Ammu, where are you?"

The tears are filling the tank to ignite all my love.
The life I craved for is burned up,
And exhausting with all her memories.
All my emotions are asking me to throttle fast,
Sharp boulders peeling the tires of my heart.

All of a sudden, there is a humpy speed breaker, I didn't notice it because of my turned head. I slam the sudden break, but it's too late, the moment is completely out of my control, the powered wheel skidded, my body and the helmet screeching against the road along with my heavy heart.

The pain became more and more, shot from my legs and the shoulder, I was thrown off near the pavement from my bike. The drops of rain taking my bloods off. I could hear the sounds of screaming people, rushing towards me. Now the pain is more and more, mentally and physically, both the pain tormenting my soul. My bike wheels are spinning and absorbing all my consciousness.

Flushes of my love screeches,
Now, my body is just a skeleton,
Twisted and thrown off.
The life of mine sucks,
Sucks hard!
To be real in this World.

My vision is getting blurred, my body is being pulled by an intangible force. Each second of my breath struggling and asking me,

'Where is your Ammu?'

'Why did she leave you alone?'

When heart is full of pain,
Mind will be full of stress,
Stress will pound the heart,
Pain will be intense in the mind.

Chapter-12

Drops of Love

"Mathav, I'm here, your love is here!"
He is screaming for help. As I open my eyes, the echo of my voice is lingering around my room walls. It's a dream in the morning after our breakup.

The colors of our love fads in the dark clouds. My heart is pounding each second that I made the wrong decision. I went in front of the mirror to see my ugly face. I felt disgusted at each glance. I ask the mirror, by touching the shadows of my own reflection.

'Is my love true?'

'There is no fault in his pure heart!!'

'Why did I break him?'
'Why did I break his dreams?'

I trust him, I trust him blindly but the questions and my insecurity conflict frequently from my intrusive thoughts. I'm a normal human, I have to solve it myself, rather than being annoyed.

The solution might be simple as I analyzed or I could have told all my fluctuations and pains. But I'm traumatized by the situations around me, Mathav or my family. Emotionally, I'm not strong enough to handle this moment and it made me think in a distinct way and hurt him from the bottom of my heart. I regret that I made a big mistake in my life.

The mirror reflects to contemplate the depth of his love, as we lived blindly for the year.

His love and care stabbed my heart,
His tears of pain swabbed my soul.

I can realize my pretentious words by the depth of his love. I whisper in front of the mirror, "Mathav I'm sorry" and my eyes cry at my own reflection that I made the wrong decision.

I had no idea how I would see him once again?
To tell him, 'Sorry!'
To plead with him, 'Sorry!'

I want his love, his pure love.

Again, to requite as a new chapter of our book. "Mathav, I'm sorry," I whisper around myself. Then, I tapped my mobile and called him, his mobile was switched off. I thought he was busy with his work. I kept trying every hour, but there was no response from him.

Late evening, I climbed to the terrace, the clouds were in the dark shades, resembling of heavy rain. The shades of clouds, telling me that "Mathav is waiting for you."

Thereafter, there is a thunderstorm, lightning is crossing my eyes. Just after a minute it starts raining heavily. I ran fast inside my home and stood near the window to stare at the unvoiced clouds, the drops of rain sprinkling from the side wall.

The sharp tone of my mobile notification echoes in the room. I urge myself that it's from Mathav. I swipe eagerly on the screen. But it's a message from Rahul.

"Thara…. Mathav met with an accident!"
"Admitted in Domlur Manipal hospital"
"Please, come fast"

In an instant, my heart skipped its beat. The word grips my shoulders. A kind of pain hitting my chest and the heart is rushing for him. My eyes are getting blurred by the tears, my body is pulling with an intangible force. The message is incomplete. I step out too fast to reach the hospital with my trembling legs.

When heart is full of pain,
Mind will be full of stress,
Stress will pound the heart,
Pain will be intense in the mind.

In front of my eyes, the roads are wide and filled with an unimaginable grief. The sky became darker and darker from the other horizon. I made a huge mistake. I couldn't forsake him all alone and hustled myself that "I betrayed his pure love, broke all his emotions and faith." Everything happened because of my impassive decisions. I pleaded my love and cried hard in the auto. "God, forgive all my mistakes."

I was trying to call Rahul to enquire about Mathav's health, but I couldn't reach his mobile. I was praying all the way that nothing serious should happen to him.

After reaching the hospital, I ran fast to the reception area near the left of the corridor and I enquired with the receptionist. She told me to hold on for a moment. She called someone and later with the hushed voice instructed me, "Take a right and straight, mam!" She guided me to the operation theater. Her face showed that he was in a serious situation.

My mind is spinning with thoughts of Mathav. I rush and stomp my hard legs on the floor by holding on to hope on the edge of the world. White lights on the narrow floors are guiding me to see my Mathav.

Rahul is waiting near the corner of the door. The sign of "Operation Theater" glitching my eyes, I ran fast and pulled his hand, Rahul "What happened to him, how is he now?"

"I don't know Thara."

His deep pitched tone is the answer to know how serious he is. Through the small glass partition, I could see the nurse and doctors covered with their scrubs and gloves, holding surgical instruments in their hands. They were hustling their rhythm along with the monitor beeps, the volume of their language was thin in the air. Mathav falls asleep in another world under the sedation.

My wrong decision, took Mathav to this serious condition, everything happened because of me. His tormenting situation is painful and no one in this world will forgive me. I sat on the chair along the wall. Each second, the pain was getting unbearable.

Rahul steps towards me and he tries to console, "Don't worry Thara, he will be alright, Let's wait!" I'm unclear and clueless. Again, I walk near to the door and I raise my head through the small glass partitions. The fragility of life comes in an unexpected way. In my mixed tears, I start to pray silently to all the Gods for his recovery.

After one hour, the doctor steps out in a comfortable manner. I stand in the hope mixed with fear in my eyes. Rahul with his hush voice,
"Is he alright, doctor?"
"What about his condition?"
I rely on the doctor, with the expectation of the boon for the rest of my life.

With a grace in the face, he began his words, "He is safe now. But there is a small fracture in his leg, we have done a minor surgery, it will take some time for recovery. Don't worry, he is alright. You can see him after he is shifted to the recovery room."

My relief washes over and my prayers are answered. I thanked the doctor and took a seat peacefully with a profound sense of strength. I don't have any hope that will glue our broken hearts. But I want a small smile on his dimpled cheek. I want him to be a happy man in this world and I want to make all my love stay alive in his heart. Around late night, he is moved to the recovery room. With my guilty walk, I slowly step inside the room.

His eyes are still closed, there are a lot of scratches on his legs and hands. The beep sound of the monitor is clinching more than Mathav's heartbeat.

As I go near him, his hand is trying to play the bow, his eyes scrunching for all the beats, his deep breath wavering in the melodic rhythm. From his semitone voice, he struggles to bridge the chords,

"Ammu!"
"Ammu!"

His voice draws me, I grab his hand fast and hold it tighter, "Mathav. I came. You are alright now."

Both his mental and physical pain, rip's my heart. The tears from his eyes dropping one by one on the blue pillow. With his tormenting voice,
"Ammu, please don't leave me alone."

"No Mathav, I won't do it anymore."

I wiped all his tears and made him relax. But his tears of pain and vulnerability pulled at my guilt.

"Mathav, sorry, I'm really sorry."

His silence filled the gap. Apart from my guilt and apology, I don't have anything to pay him. The anguish of remorse is hurting me more and more. I don't have any other words which could soothe him from all the pain.

Then, he draws my hands on his chest,
"It's okay, Ammu. You came back. That's enough for me. I can bear any pain in this world."
That minute, I realized that I can convince this entire universe if they are against us and with his love, I can solve everything. The only medicine I can offer him at that moment is the hope that it won't happen again. I wiped his tears once again and I kissed him on his forehead to give him hope for a new life. And the days in the hospital are filled with romance by seeing all the tablets, stretchers and the wounds. Every single second, he stays and waddles in my eyes.

I stayed with him,
Held his hands,
Massaged his feet, and
Kissed on his pain.

Served my love,
In the cup of juices.

Served my love,
With the pieces of fruit.

Served my love,
From the sheets of the tablet.

Served my love,
As an antibiotic for his wounds.

And I served my love,
In the words of hope and care.

I served everything which I could offer him for the recovery. After two days, the doctor asked him to practice walking by using the crutches. He begins the hard step of his life. Step by step, he crosses all his hard days and the painful life. I know it's very difficult to manage him all alone and there is nobody to take care of him. After he was discharged, I took him home. With the help of Rahul, we vacated all his room.

The new life for us just started with hope. I started to serve all my love in place of his parents. Day by day, I could see the improvement in his health and an energy in his walk. His brave smile teaches me a lot about life. I love him from dusk to dawn. I love him.

Gravity, you lost to pull my body,
As 'she is my melody.'

Chapter-13

She is my Melody

My recovery is fast in Thara's hands, all my wounds are healing by her care and our love is growing in the other corner. With her intensive love, every wound loses its life. New skin regenerates. The hard part of our story is to imagine how we loved each other by every means, the hidden love.

One fine evening, after my day nap, I step out of the room. I feel her absence, my eyes are searching all the corners and I rush my voice,

"Ammu, Ammu…. Where are you?"

"Mathav, I'm here." the voice rings from the kitchen. As I reach the kitchen. Her eyes are searching the rows of ingredients bottles, "Ammu, what are you searching for?"

Her little voice pitches out, "Uff, I found this garam masala."

"Do you want any help?" I asked her.

"No Mathav, I will manage, you take rest."

"Ammu, I'm tired of taking rest, please let me do something!"

"Hmm okay yaar, tell me what you want to do?" she shrugs.

"Today, I will help you, Ammu. What are you planning to cook for dinner?"

"Vegetable rice!!"

"Cool. Then, I will cut these vegetables" and I grab a knife from the holder which is mounted on the wall.

"Okay" she nodded and began to peel off the outer layers of it and I picked those to chop it off. Quickly, with her crunchy voice, "Mathav, I have to ask you one thing."

Her eyes are holding some mysteries, the voice hangs in the semitones. Did she forget the recipe or something to buy? I ask her, "What happened Ammu, do you forget anything to buy?"

She murmurs, "No, it's not."

Still, there is something in her mind which is hesitant to come out. Her eyes are humming and hawing between the peeler and the vegetables.
"What? Ammu, tell me." I try to pull her oscillating mind.

"Mathav, I'm planning to visit my home. My mom and sister are alone now. I feel like spending some more time with them and kind of taking a break from my work, Shall I go?"

The very next second. I said, "Of course Ammu, you can. I will never stop you for anything that really matters to you."

"Mathav, but you will be alone here! That's my worry and it's hesitating me to take the decision. I don't want to leave you alone."

"Ammu! "I'm completely recovered now. I will take care of myself. You don't get confused, it's just for some days. Definitely I will miss you but anyway, I will not be alone, your memories are behind these walls, that's enough to wake me up. If I feel lonely, ofcourse I will call or message you the next second."

From her stuttering lips, "I know you can, but."

Still there is a bite of hesitation to leave me alone. I kept the knife on the plate and I reached close to her. I pull her hand into mine and I whisper to break her hesitation, "Don't worry Ammu."

She nods, "Okay." But her bottom of the heart is hanging by my missing melodies. I shake her trembling hand and I put my arms around her to feel light, "That's my girl." I breath in my soothing voice and the soft touch of my palm gradually relaxes her mind.

"Thanks for understanding, Mathav." She whispers.

"I don't want thanks now, first cook me the vegetable rice." I said and I started to chop off the remaining vegetables.

"You, idiot." She laughs. In between our chuckles and
plays, we start to cook our lovable vegetable rice.

The ghee melts in the voice of her melody,
To spread the fairly aroma.
The layers of onion spatter the tears,
From the world of deep pot.
And the chopped green chilies swims in the flood,
To stay awake in her eyes.

Sweet corn on the one end,
Green capsicum on the other end,
Shares the color of our happiness.

Mushroom shows its enlightenment,
From the emerged darkness. And
The salt fades into the nerves of water,
To add savory taste to our life.

The soaked white pearls of rice,
Carries the floppy layer of wetness,
And the utter fragrance of her.

The magic of vegetable rice,
Flushes up from the epidermis.
The chopped vegetables around the world,
Blends the beautiful color for our life.

And dinner is added to the plates,
The music show played on the TV,
The warm light embraces us.

By sitting on the two corners of sofa,
We served our food,
In sweet nourish,
By each bite,
With deep love.

Yes, we served our love,
In the art of cooking, And
In the magic of vegetable rice.

Cooking is an art where she is my artist to blend the taste for it. Every art piece of hers is my favorite and every stroke of the ladle is her unique style. All the aroma measures the magic of her fragrance and it may fade every day, nevertheless the life of art is infinite. The taste buds of my mouth exude the taste of her art in every second of my life. Yes, the life of her art is infinite.

While chewing the last bite, she whispers, "Mathav, I have one surprise for you,"

"Is it really?" my excitement hangs all the rice on my upper mouth.

"Yeah!" she grins.

"What is that?"

"Wash your hands, I will tell you"

"Keep this plate." I handed it to her and flew at the speed of hypersonic to wash my hands inside the kitchen and I rushed back to the hall with the towel in my hand and wiped it promptly.

"Ammu, I'm ready. What is the surprise?" I ask her.

"Hey you, kiddy, I will tell you after you wash this plate" she tries to hallucinate my excitement.

After taking the plate from her and quickly washing it, I brought her a wash bowl because I know what she will ask me to do next. I carry it near the sofa and I nail my legs down to her.

"Ammu, here is a wash bowl, wash your hands. I can't wait long, please tell me."

She laughs at my 12-year kiddy excitement. I can pretend as much as I want but my heart can't, with the loved one. My art of love is being playful with her and showing her how much I mean to her.

"Come on, let's go my boy." She takes me to the balcony. Under the dark night, I couldn't see anything properly. Mysteries are added in the black colors. She holds my left arm and her soft touch is waiting to see my excitement.

"Mathav, switch on this button," She hands me a small remote. Despite the dark night, my vision is immersed by the light of green in it. A small button on the top and I pressed it.

The warm yellow fairy lights are curved in the symbol of our heart and hang to the sides of the wall. The germinated seeds on the pot peeks outside to see the love of our life and the greenery of the money plant shines in the color of love. My pretty girl with an open heart is welcoming the glow. There is a small wooden easel stand at the corner of the balcony where it's completely covered with red cloth.

"Ammu, what is this?" my excitement in the warm light glimmered more than the scattered light.

She heads up and grins, "Open and see!"

I walked closely and pulled the red cloth. As I draw it from the bottom, my eyes take in the painting frame by frame, my heart is beating with a deep, deep pound. The sound of it reaches my ears.

"Oh My God, it's amazing," I'm enthralled and stand numb to the mesmerizing painting.

It's me with my friend on the vibrant stage, my one hand with the bow and the other hand with his body. Two sides with a half hanging curtain, my pretty girl with the microphone. Under the dark stage, the corner lights focus on us in the sync of our melody. My eyes winked by welcoming our evoking show, *The Art of Our Melody.*

I turn my head to her, she looks vivacious, "Ammu, I love this and it's the best surprise I've ever received after my violin."

She grins in the magic of love and by seeing my flying heart. I clasp her arms under me and ask, "Did you paint this?"

In her semitone she whispers, "Ya."

Then, she gasps, "Mathav, do you remember? Long back you asked me about my wishes. This is one of the wishes, Mathav. I have to sing to your tune on the big stage, in front of thousands of enchanting people."

For a few seconds, I stood speechless. Is this life really tendering the great things? She gave me all and everything. In the existence she is my dream, her wish is our melody. I'll do anything for her, now her wish is my dream. In a surprised note, I mumble. "Ammu, now It's my dream, the day is getting closer."

"Is it? If this happens, I will be the happiest person in this world."

My music and my love changed my life for the better and better than I ever expected and experienced. At that second, my heart pumps only for her, which tells me that the day is today. My dream pulls my words from the heart,

"Ammu, Let's do it now."

"Really? How?" She is delighted.

"Ya, will not wait for the thousands of people, let's give the soul to all the inanimate worlds."

"Mathav, I'm ready." She reflects my love in her cute smile. And she ran fast to pick my violin. My love of life in her hand, getting me started on our enchanting show *"The Art of Our Melody."* I took my violin to start, the happiness in her eyes enlightens our fairy world. Then,

The butterflies start to dance in the sky,
Where I laid my leg down to fly.
Gravity, Pull my heart,
She wants to find my thoughts.

Her pretty strings hover,
My soul is connected with quaver,
She tunes my adoring peg,
Vibrations wince on my leg,

I start with my bow,
♫...... ♫....... ♫..... ♫

She pours her love with the snow...
♫.....♫..... ♪...... ♪.....♫..... ♫

Then I play her breathe of life...
♫.....♫..... ♪...... ♫..... ♫...... ♪.....♫..... ♫

She adds colors to our life...
♫…..♫….. ♪…… ♪…..♫….. ♫

My play fogs our fairy wonderland.
♫…… ♫……. ♫….. ♫

And her pretty voice adds melody to our heaven.
♫…..♫….. ♪…… ♪…..♫….. ♫

Our melody continued for a while in her voice and the play of my friend. Our dreamy show ends, she hugs me in the showers of flowers from our fairy world.

"Mathav, now I'm the happiest person and can die in this second." Her smile mixed with the tears of love. She slightly sobs at our harmonizing melody and she puts her head on my chest. Hugging by an unbreakable bond around my waist. I rush my hand finding its way to her hair, comforting all her heartfelt emotions.

The growth of love is sharing every mixed emotion. I'm not a lackluster to treat all her emotions, the word ego is not derived in my life dictionary, then how could I disregard her affection and unsaid emotions. My respect is not just for her love, its more than that and it's quite difficult to describe in a word.

I ask, "Ammu, are you happy?"

"Mathav what else do I need?"

Her love drops from her eyes and sprinkles on the withered flowers of my heart. With mixed emotions, her voice stammers, "Mathav…I love you." She closes my heart and completes my story by hugging with her profound love.

I'm wrestling to find my words to bridge her emotions. There is no force in this world to pull her hug, my piece of life tied a knot in her dreamy land with the affirmations of the skies. Her utter affection forces and spins this earth at more than the speed of 1000 miles per hour.

Gravity, you lost to pull my body,
As 'she is my melody.'

"Ammu, it's okay," the voices from my closed heart pampering her and lulling her. Then I lift her face in my palm and kiss on her forehead. The connection of our love electrifies her eyes. Her eyes, the mesmerizing eyes pulls my body, the gravity lost its law on this earth. It's not the same as 9.81 m/s^2. Nevertheless, it's beyond the law of attraction.

The intangible force pulls us inside the room, all my energy pulls down from my legs. Finally, I'm numb, not in any way to recognize myself. Lost in her, lost in this earth. Inside the wall of our fairy room, in between the frames, our eyes stare for a minute and she slowly kisses on my lips. From her cheek, my fingers are lost between her ear and the curly hair. Her hand on my cheek softens my breath. I slowly kissed her lip and tasted her love. It's a desert full of water. From the slope of bare peaks, my lips completely drench inside it. I breathe her warm breath and she breathes my warm breath. After passionate kissing,

My hands on her neck slowly removes all her octaves,
The music ends but our melody starts,
The notes of our lips transferring down,

Kisses from the lips to the neck,
And from the neck to the chest.

All my ten fingers joined with the ten keys,
The warm chorus twirls us.
I played the sharp notes,
Our hearts joined in the rhythm.

The semitones drawn from our breathe,
The hot air mixed in the tempo.

In the deep track,
The beautiful song shared between us.

My soul pats near her chinrest,
My body on her upper bout,
And my bow crossed between our legs.

Our beautiful melody ends with the tears in the corner of my eyes. The true love of us brought me happy tears. We both on the bed and her head on my arms, silence is the only language between us. I love the warm melody of us. After relaxing ourselves. I ask her, "Ammu, do you believe in reincarnation?"

She asks me, "Why?"

Her question doubts beyond the horizon, face implies that she's wondering why I'm asking her an unrealistic question of life in this eternity. Her eyes blink clueless.

"Tell me," I said.

"No, I don't think so."

"But I do Ammu. I think I'm mad about the unrealistic life and moreover I want to live with you indefinitely."

"You are crazy" she loves all my stupid things.

"It's my love Ammu. You know, if anyone asked me before seeing you, I could have said, 'No'. But after realizing our life I need it badly."

She grins as if showing her love more than what she thinks. "You are my everything Mathav."

My crazy love tells me to think and make her a queen of my moon land. Where I just took a minute to think about the state of reincarnation. Everything wants me to stay with her forever in this universe.

I mean, in everything.

As an earring for her ears,
As an anklet for her legs,
As a mirror for her beauty.

As a nail on her hands,
As a hair on her head,
As a skin on her bones.

As a sweat on her neck,
As an odor on her shoulder.

As a pillow for her sleep,
As a tablet for her fever,
And, as a grass for her feet.

In her arm, the sun rises from the horizon, from the search for her to with her, with her completely, with her naked. My heart soars over the sky as no one can express my happiness other than her. The queen of my life completes me and the reason for my birth. The fact that she is leaving Bangalore for some days, makes me somewhat sad. But I won't stop her in any case, but my mind pretends to do so I'm gonna miss her for some days.

The next evening, she packs all her dresses in the big suitcase for her flight and waits for the cab in the hall. Almost she is ready to leave, my face turns dull and my words in semitone.

She asks, "Mathav, are you okay?"

"Ya, I'm good" I pretended to be fine for her.

"Mathav, I know it's about our long distance, don't worry I will come back soon."

"Okay" I whisper.

She took a step to give me a warm cuddle to reflect her missing me. The soft hug relaxes me and my sense of wanting her increases. Under my arm, her phone buzzes.

"Mathav, cab arrived. I have to leave now," she says. I came down with her by descending the heavy steps. The car driver opens the boot. She kept all her luggage into it. And she took a seat near the window to tell me hard goodbyes.

"Mathav, bye. Take care."

"Bye Ammu. Stay safe." My voice cries inside me.

I recovered from all the miseries and the pain which was unfortunate. It's difficult to stare at the walls with memories running in my head but I accept everything, because it's all for her and my art of love is merely for her.

Is there anyone,
To rewrite my stories,
And my happiness?

Chapter-14

Final Message

Thara, my eternal beauty.
Her presence is my only breath to feel, I'm not heavy and I'm a normal person to live my life. The situation around me is rehabilitating that I could thank God for offering me more and more pain, which always turns into the happiest moments of my life.

After reaching her home, the text "Mathav, I reached safely" washes over my big anticipation. We are around 2000 kms apart, but the distance feels like she stays on a different planet that I can't travel easily. My life is not easy without Thara, I start to count all my endless days, however the pampering messages from far distances keeps my heart calm and to battle with my flow.

Two weeks later, early in the morning, I got a call from Lipsa, that she will be coming home in the next hour to pick up her left-out luggage. After that she said, "Mathav, I have to tell you an important thing." Her voice carries a hint of some pain. But my mind is not surprised by anything, as she is coming here to pick her stuff. Around afternoon I took a lengthy seat on the sofa to watch Thara's concert videos on TV. Her melodies are the ones which make me snap my ears throughout 86400 seconds of the day. Despite her absence, the essence of her cooking still floats around the walls.

Soon after, the doorbell bashes my ears, I open the door slowly, the cranky sound under niching on the floors, with a sad face and hollowed eyes, her face holds thousands of mysteries. Now the excitement looms large on my face, I ask Lipsa.

"Are you okay?"

In her trembling voice, "Mathav, I am sorry." The unsaid word creates tension around me. Each second slows down the beat of my heart. My heart carries the thin suffocated air.

"What happened?" I ask her as my heart skips a beat. A second of silence flashes on Lipsa's face, with her stammering words and a small drop of tear in the corner of eyes.

"Thara is no more."

My body shatters for a second and froze. I say, "What are you saying? Don't play with me Lipsa!"

"Mathav, please believe me" she sobs.

The words are like cracks spreading on the tectonic plates of my heart, inducing pain so deep and deep. The tears start to flood from my eyes, the air becomes dense and heavy around me, the suffocation is spreading over the floors. I'm losing my strength and I fall on the floor, yearning for her arms. My hand is in the air, craving to see her cute face, longing to hear her voice and the world of her eyes.

Every wall of Thara's house echoes with a deafening silence. Her frame in the hall falls on the floor and breaks into uncountable pieces. The knives in her kitchen, battle each other to lose their sharp life. The strings of my violin screech in my ear.

"Thara is no more."

Lipsa was too dumbstruck with her words to console me, even her heart was carrying the heavy grief, we are staring at each other with the rivers of tears in our eyes. She raises me from the floor to the sofa, my contracted muscles cramp, my leg winces by the broken skeleton. She sits near me and puts her hands on my shoulder to show her pity but literally she feels disheartened on seeing me.

There is a small part of my heart hoping that she is still alive. Somewhere she is still alive. Our love is infinite and it will never fade easily. I collect some hope for living again. I stood from the sofa and I wiped my tears.

"She said that she will come back, my Ammu is still alive Lipsa, come let's go and see."

"Mathav, please if you can't control and feel lost, it's okay to be." She wrenches my pain.

"No Lipsa, she is waiting for me, don't say this again!" my voice is little above my tone. Clashing in the battle to find my queen.

"Mathav, it's okay, relax, relax."

Her voice is breaking between the barriers. A heavy silence fills the room in the sounds of our pain. Its bashing among the four walls and moving around us. In between the sounds of clock, Tick, Tick. I lose the hope of winning my life battle. Kneeling down on the floor, I cry on losing everything. The color of pain leeches on the floor. After battling with the reality that "she is no more."

I ask, "Lipsa what happened to her all of a sudden?"

She lifts her breath in the intensity of loss, "Her sister informed me that she was going through 'Takotsubo cardiomyopathy' which is why she got a sudden heart attack last night."

"Lipsa, I don't know what you are telling me exactly, what is that? She was good here. She was happy here" I sob.

She whispers, "Mathav, I don't even know what really happened. Everything seems mysterious."

"Why us?" I bawl in the profound loss of her.

My words are mixed with the rain of tears to digest it. Her unsaid words blend in the anguish of loss. The reality has no eyes to see my gloomy life. The pain scratches the flushes from my skin and now I'm dead mentally with just bones in my body.

Smile on my face,
Love in my eyes,
Dimple cheeks,
Dance on the floors

But the mystery is,
'My life is invisible'
And not my own, it was
My only reflection.

I lost my love,
My smile,
My dimple,
My dance
And my melody.

Now, anger on the face,
Fluttery eyes,
Fearful knees,
My heart's mirror is broken.

Suddenly, my mind remembered her personal diary, that she might have mentioned everything about herself. I ran inside the bedroom. I start to search on her tables and racks. I couldn't find it anywhere. Later I pull out the draw, down towards the table, there is a brown leather diary. I picked it up and started to turn the hard cover. Inside the bumpy clouds, *"The Art of Our Melody"* was written in bold.

I turn to the next page of her diary. It starts with our first meeting. In the pages of clouds, our beautiful meeting is sketched on one side and those memories are written on the other side. I start to read every page, an unconditional bond of feelings floods inside me. The pages are reminding me and taking me back with her through the chapters of the early stories. Chai days to church street, Lahe Lahe and the long walk with her. All those memorable chapters of our stories deepens my vulnerability, But the reality hits me more… that "Thara is not alive."

In the middle of her diary, the chapter which was detailed and highlighted in bumpy clouds, "My Last Wish."

I shout, "Lipsa, Lipsa, she wrote about her Last wish." I felt something mysterious that she wrote her last wish in the diary. It hampers me that she was undergoing some difficult phase which was not shared with anyone. I lift my right hand and wipe the shedding tears on my face.

She runs fast to my voice and by holding the door, "Mathav, read, read it," she urges me to read that Thara might have notified everything over there.

Mathav, I'm writing this, as your love brought me endless happiness in my life. Since the day you asked me about my wishes, I have been thinking more about my last wish. After sharing my life, I found my dream in you and the question of my last wish is scanty which lies in you and with you. That's my daily prayer too, 'Your astounding melodies are what the world wants to hear'. Never give up your art, play your soulful melodies to this beautiful world and evoke everyone's love and hope for their life. The love in you which made me love you.

If my diary finds you after my death. For me, for your Ammu, don't let your tears flow away. Attend my funeral in your favourite white shirt and play your favourite melody. All I want is to hear every part of your art even after death. By relaxing with you, dancing with you and singing with you. Play it loudly, where no one can hear from outside of our hearts. If you ever find yourself missing me eternally, pull your friend Mathav, I'm your melody coming out to sweep all the pain of this world, and to spread the love beyond the horizon.

As I turn the pages of my clouds, tears are filling and smudging with her memories. She recorded all her love till our cooking night. After that, the pages are empty, again I didn't get any clue about what happened to her? she didn't mention it anywhere, mysteries are hidden with her. Now, all our beautiful stories are just a book in this unknown world. No one will read it until you share this unsaid story, my Thara's story, my Ammu's story.

Stories of my breath,
Lasted,
Buried with her, and
Smudging in my tears,

Is there anyone,
To wipe our chapters,
And our pages?

Is there anyone,
To rewrite our stories,
And our happiness?

Is there anyone,
To kiss our context
And hug our book?

Is there anyone?

The connection of pain in my story is punching my heavy heart and pulling down the pain. Without any clue and a profound loss, I lift my face to Lipsa, a deep sense of sorrow even in her eyes searching for the unsaid words.

A minute later she whispers, "Mathav, come let's go and attend her funeral, we can find out what happened to her? What was she going through?" I took a deep breath. One side I needed to search her mysteries and the other side her last wish. Both of this, pulls my legs to move out and moreover the honour of my love is to respect and pay her the last wish.

I kept her diary in my bag, which is a treasure and the memories of our love. And I pack my small luggage to attend her funeral.

We both boarded, in search of Thara's life story.

My stubborn heart,
Needs her reincarnation.

Chapter-15

Reincarnation

As we soar over the sky, my love falls down from the clouds to say, 'Sorry'. The love beyond the mountains and the clouds stays at an unreachable point. I turn my head towards the window, looking out at the clouds that my search for the last pages is still alive and unsaid.

People who say they are strong, are really not, they are hiding their pain, to enlighten their well-being. Even I did the same. I pretended to be brave in other's eyes, but all my emotions were spineless and scared. It's difficult to live with the pain again and again. And it's tormenting me more.

I asked for a normal life, normal life like others, but not for unusual pain, which is more than that of normal people.

Delusion is,
Neither heart nor mind.
In the subconscious distress,
Pain is inevitable.

By the time we reached, all the final funeral rituals were completed. We were late to reach, but to fulfill her last wish, Lipsa and I walked towards Thara's cremation. I wore my favorite white shirt. I stepped closer to my love, she is sleeping inside the world with immersed beauty, The moon and the sun both rise up to show their grief. I couldn't control my loss. But for her, the wall in my eyes blocks all the flooding tears. My heart pounds down to control its heart beat.

"Ammu, wake up from your sleep, I came to see you"

I kneel down to her and I pull my bow on one hand. My violin rests between my chin and my shoulder, her strength supports my bow to hold it tight. In my eyes, she lifts her soul up from the cremation site and she starts to sing for my melody. Her voice rises above the sea. *"Tu Hi Re"* composed by AR Rahman, I play it by controlling all my breath and I plead in my melody,

"Ammu, one last time, come in front of me, my eyes are longing to see you."
"Ammu, my stubborn heart needs your reincarnation! Where are you?" my melody shouts out on this world.

My stubborn heart,
Needs your reincarnation
To pat my head,
On your shoulder,

My stubborn heart,
Needs your reincarnation
To share my love,
In your arms.

My stubborn heart,
Needs your reincarnation
To play my melody
In your singing.

My stubborn heart,
Needs your reincarnation
To live my life,
In your chastity.

Ammu, my stubborn heart,
Needs your Reincarnation.

I try to control all the miserable pain in between my melodies. The voice of Thara's sister screaming from far behind, "Bhai! Bhai!"

Her voice holding some stories to share with me. And I stopped my melody, as she is approaching us.

At that second, I found a big hope that Thara's is still alive. The clouds of the gloomy sky open his hands to shower me the truth.

She rushes fast towards me and positions herself, "Bhai…" She breathes heavily to pick the unsaid words.

My heart speaks silently and holds those mysteries in her eyes. She whispers,

"Bhai, I want to tell you something important," her heart pounds faster than her words. Everything around me freezes for the message that she carried.

She sobs, "Bhai, she didn't tell anyone what happened to her. No one knows. For the past week she has not been okay. She isolated herself at home and avoided talking with everyone. Yesterday afternoon she left home alone, and in the evening we got a call that she was serious and was admitted to a hospital. I went to see her. She was struggling to speak and did not reveal anything personal. By holding her half breath, she wrote this letter and handed it to me to give to you in any case. Doctor was saying something like 'Takotsubo cardiomyopathy' but we are waiting for the postmortem report."

With no clue even from her sister, I felt disheartened about this life. I don't know what else she was undergoing that made her not disclose it with anyone.

"Bhai, this is the letter," she raised her hand towards me. In the fraction of second, I pick it up from her hands and start to read it.

All her words are again mysteries and I didn't get what happened to her really? But something she was undergoing was bad that proffered in her painful writings. In her every word she carried a loss.

Everything else fades by the letter, *The Art of Our Melody,* which she mentioned hauls my breathe.

Again, my heart asks, "God, why is it for us?"

I'm speechless. Damn Speechless by her letter. Realizing that she is no more, the pressurized blood from my broken heart pumps and scatters as the glass pieces and it's screeching in my veins. My eyes pull all the scattered blood as a tear.

The violin falls from my hand. By holding the pain in my heart, I kneel down on the broken mirrors. My heart stops its pounding. I can feel that the breath fades slowly from me. The art of leaving my breath. Now mentally and physically, I'm dead inside the circle of the mirror.

Now, the mirror stabbed my heavy heart and broke it into uncountable pieces. It's no use living again. All the pampering of my love splits in all the four directions and scatters back to the sky.

If you collect all the broken pieces of my art, it may be the beautiful painting in the wall of your heart. But all I want is, let it be a story in my heart and as a novel on your table.

Chapter-16

The Last Page of Clouds

All my broken mirrors are observed by the external gravity, which lost its pull on my body. The next morning, I woke up from the new mirror. Everything around me is colorful to my eyes. The new fairy world is surrounded by white and pink blossoms. I could see the beautiful butterflies flying all around.

But this time, my heart is light, it feels cheerful. As all my Ammu's love has changed me to a cheerful person in my last birth. Similar to my last birth, I started to stare at the sky as a 12-year boy. It feels like I'm going to see my Ammu again and live my previous life with her.

While seeing the moving clouds, I could hear the melody of "My heart will go on" from afar.

"Where is it from?" my anticipation draws my legs to search. I start to run towards the soothing melody.

The heartwarming melody took me to the lands of our fairy world. The green bushes colored with the yellow flowers. My pink blossoms are blooming around the path. I feel extremely happy that in my new world, it blooms entire seasons and it's going to stay with me.

The melody took my heart to reach under a perennially blooming tree that resembles the place where my mom teaches me music and where it is crowded by the green enchanting leaves. But here, the violin is playing by a little girl with feathers on her back. She plays the melody in the art of living and in rebirth. It is enchanting to my soul. In every scale, she sharpens the notes of melody. From behind the tree, I start to walk around it to see her face.

As I walk infront of her, she stops her beautiful play. The small butterfly flutters down and lands gently on the girl's outstretched shoulder. Her cute angelic smile lights the fairy world. Beside the cute girl, my pretty love, my Thara, my Ammu. On seeing me again in the new world, my Thara's eyes glimmer, the wide smile from us showers the pink blossoms from the trees. For a second, the frame of our new world moves around us. My happiness is endless, staring at her and seeing her once again in this heaven.

My heart jumps down on heaven and asks my Ammu with great excitement about the cute girl.

"Who is this cute girl? Ammu." I ask her.

Her happy face widened my heart and brought me meaning for the lost life.

"She is, the art of our melody"
"Our daughter, Mathav."

The word froze me for a minute, her cute angelic smile rewinds the memories of Thara's last letter, where clouds move and laps on it fast to show me the last page,

Dear my love,

In the last week of time, a lot of things happened around me which no one should come across. I thought of surprising you and beginning our new life, but everything changed after reaching Delhi. I didn't expect my life to change like that. Mathav, "I'm sorry." I'm not strong like you. People around me destroyed my life and our love.

Mathav, I love you more and more, that's the reason may be, I found your last page of clouds before my last breath.

Yes, love of our life became meaningful,
'The Art of Our Melody'
I'm pregnant, Mathav.
I'm pregnant.

My heart cries in the pain, but the smiles on the cute little girl wonders in my eyes. In her sweet voice she calls me, "Papa."

My happy tears reach my hand. I'm numb from the profound loss of my Ammu and my daughter in my last birth. But the last page of clouds is written so beautifully in my story, *"The Art of Our Melody."*

I run to her and lift her high in between the magical space. I outstretch my arms and I twirl her around me. The pure joy and connection creates an endless life on our moonland. After spinning around the space, I hugged her and kissed my daughter in the love of living again. My Ammu sees our play by standing beside us. On seeing her, I stretch my arms. She walks close to me. I cuddle her under my arms. I twirl her curly hair and I kiss her head.

The next minute, The sound of 'Bow! Bow!' from behind the tree pulls our attention. My Ammu starts to search for the cute voice. As we walk close to the tree, the puppy with wounded right eye isn't aware of what happened to her in her early life. The other eye stings in the tears, I can feel the same pain as mine.

As we step in front of the puppy, the pretty little face lifts up showing the life in the mixed eyes, "Is there anything to heal me?" the puppy asks.

We knelt our legs down to shower all the flowers from our hearts. My Ammu lifts the puppy up in her hands. The cute puppy licks her face and kisses on her chin.

Yes. Our heart is here.
And our unsaid words are here.

Then,
'*My Pinky*' on my left hand,
'*Cute Puppy's*' rope leash on her left hand,
'*The Art of Our Melody*' on my right hand,
'*My friend*' on her right hand.
We start our new beginnings, which are endless and infinite in this universe.

I love the hope of being loved.

"The True Love of Withered Flowers"

Ponderings….

- Do you think Mathav found a perfect partner for his life?
- How would Thara's life have changed if she had not met Lipsa?
- What if he had gotten a friend like Rahul during his school time? What happened to Mathav throughout his school days?
- Who is Rahul? Where did he leave off in the middle of the story?
- Do you think the character 'Mathav' is a real person? If you found a boy who loves you like Mathav does, would you propose to him?
- Who are Mathav's biological parents? Where is he from?
- What happened to Thara's brother? Why did he kill himself? Is suicide the only way to fix his problems?
- From when did Thara suffer from Takotsubo Cardiomyopathy? Is it really true? What is written in the postmortem report?
- What happened to the wounded right eye puppy?
- Why did Thara's family move to Delhi after her father's death? Why didn't Thara's mother think about remarriage? Is it society or love?
- What happened to Thara? Why did she go back to Delhi? What happened in the last week? Why didn't she disclose it to anyone? Why did she isolate herself at home?

Keep an eye out for my series...

To Open Your Heart!

- Is it good to live without understanding the other side of a person?
- If you find yourself lacking belongings and love, what will you do?
- How will you treat your partner when they are in pain?
- When you grow up with all the love and belongings except wealth, how will you face this world?
- The term "People of Wealth" just serves as an attraction. Do you agree?
- Do you love the hope of being loved?
- If you were a parent, how would you teach your child about love?
- When you lose all your love and affection, how will you drive your life?
- When you find yourself in a state of confusion, how will you choose to resolve it?
- Do you comprehend the meaning of love? Are you seeing it from your partner? If not, did you expect that? If that expectation fails, does your understanding of love remain correct?
- And finally, do you find what is love?

About Author

Rajesh Rajavelu is an author, artist and poet. From his childhood days, he had a passion for the music, art and writings. He studied Mechanical Engineering and to pursue his career, he moved to Bangalore, India. Later on, he started to explore his passion. In the name of 'Majeev Arts' he created plenty of happiness among the people. His motivation for creating the art is not merely to achieve something big, it's about giving a love and the hope for everyone's life.

For Rajesh, he never wants to leave this world. In the name of 'Art', he desired immortality.

To connect with the author.
Instagram: Rajesh Rajavelu (_iam_majeev)
Mail: author.rajeshrajavelu@gmail.com

www.ingramcontent.com/pod-product-compliance
Lightning Source LLC
LaVergne TN
LVHW041516170726
843492LV00005B/1530